Broker / Dealer

Tony Bailey

Table of Contents

Introduction

Introduction

Broker-Dealer (bro-ker-deal-er)

Noun - A brokerage firm that buys and sells securities on its own account as a principal before selling the securities to customers.

Will Rogers once said "Too many people spend money they haven't earned, to buy things they don't want, to impress people they don't like". Well guess what, I'm not Will Rogers and if he were here, I'd tell him to kiss my ass. I've spent a lot of money that I've worked damn hard to earn, and yes, I have also bought a shit ton of things no one ever "needs" to impress my friends and family. To be honest I don't care if you like me, because as a wise group once said, "cash rules everything around me, cream, get the money, dolla dolla bills ya'll". Yes I'm quoting the Wu Tang Clan because they gave us the best quote of all time, plus those are the words I live by, each and every day. You're probably thinking, this guy's an asshole, but I wasn't always a money hungry, materialistic prick that only cares about himself and his net worth, I was a baby at one point in my life.

Chapter 1 – Childhood

I was born in Greeley, Colorado on January 20th of 1977 and I grew up in a middle class family with two loving parents, Steve and Cindy, and my two brothers, Mark and Spencer. I'm the youngest of the three and my two older brothers always looked out for me, even though they occasionally picked on me. They would hold me down and tickle me until I literally peed myself. Mark, the middle brother, use to pin me to the ground by sitting on my chest and holding my arms above my head, he would then slowly release spit out of his mouth and would suck it back up before it fell on my face. This drove me bat shit crazy and one time he actually let it go and he spit on my face. Needless to say I went ballistic and once I was able to free myself, I got up and chased him around the house with a knife until my Mom stopped me. I was crying so hard I could barely catch my breath to explain what Mark had done. When I calmed down enough to tell her, she grounded my brother and gave me a warning for chasing him with a knife even though I said I would never hurt him. My parents were the best and they had a lot, and I mean a lot of patience with us boys.

They gave us space and the freedom to make our own choices and decisions. Sometimes we made the right choice and did great things like doing our chores and homework, and other times when we made bad choices like dumping baby oil on the kitchen floor and hallway and treating it like an in home slip and slide. We paid the price for it with a belt or a wooden spoon to the butt, mostly the fear of both was enough, but either way good or bad the choice was ours to make all on our own. Mom and Dad always said "Make good choices today so you don't have regrets tomorrow". I always regretted getting the spoon or belt, especially the day after, took a while for the soreness to go away.

Being the youngest and still in elementary school, sometimes I would tag along with my brothers. We knew all the neighborhood kids in Virginia Hills, our neighborhood in Greeley, as we would ride our bikes around the entire neighborhood and played games of tag, hide and go seek, and capture the flag. Growing up in the suburbs of Virginia Hills had its benefits as it was a quiet and peaceful town, or at least where I lived, the east side of Greeley wasn't all that safe. But to us boys it was the good ole days, get up, eat a bowl of Captain Crunch and get on the bus to go to school. There was this girl who lived across the street from me named Katie and she also went to my school. My best friend Carter and I both had a crush on her and we'd occasionally wrestle each other for her undying love, which probably never existed, but we believed she liked us both. My brother Mark knew I had a crush on her and one year the entire neighborhood, parents and kids, were standing in a giant circle in the street lighting off fireworks for the 4th of July. Katie was standing directly across from me and just as Spencer, my oldest brother lit a roman candle, Mark was behind me and he pulled down my shorts, all the way to my ankles and in the light of the fireworks, there I stood facing Katie with my shorts and underwear at my ankles, in shock, as she looked directly at me. I was mortified and quickly pulled up my tighty whiteys and shorts and ran into the house crying. Again, my brother Mark was grounded and my Mom made him apologize. He seemed sincere but I held on to that grudge for a long time even though Katie and

I continued to be friends as if nothing happened.

On the weekends my brothers and I would stay up late and play video games on the Nintendo or Atari, watch scary movies like Friday the 13th, Nightmare on Elm Street or Faces of Death, and all of us kids would meet up at the dust bowl, a large undeveloped dirt lot at the lower end of the neighborhood, which we turned into our own private BMX track. After dinner we would ride our bikes around the neighborhood all night long and at the crack of dawn we would follow the milk delivery truck around as they dropped off glass jugs of milk, blocks of cheese, and sometimes ice cream. My brothers and I, along with our friends would take the milk, cheese, and ice cream out of the milk boxes people had on their patios and we would stash all of it in the refrigerator in the basement. The basement was our recreational room and it was amazing. Mom would buy us cereal and cookies and we kept it all downstairs and when all the neighborhood kids came over we would gather in the basement to hang out and play video games and watch movies.

One Saturday we were hanging out in the basement and this kid named Travis who lives at the end of the block dared me to ride my bike down the street to the gas station on the corner, next to Monfort Elementary School, and steal as much candy as possible and bring it back to prove that I'm not a wussy. Of course I had to prove I'm not a wussy, so I took the dare and I rode my bike out of the neighborhood and down 20th Street to the corner store, wearing the biggest jacket I could find, mind you it was summer so I was sweating up a storm. My best friend Carter rode with me and said I should steal the candy when he distracted the store clerk. I asked Carter what his plan was and he replied, just wait and see. Carter walked into the store and told the clerk he needed air for his bike tire and asked the clerk to show him where the air pump was because he couldn't find it. I watched though the window and saw the clerk look around and then he walked out of the store with Carter, exiting the doors on the other side near the air pump, and that was my sign so I bolted into the store from the other door and I started taking as much candy as I could fit into my oversized coat. My hands were shaking and I was scared shitless. I was so frightened about getting caught that my nerves were on edge and I thought I heard them coming back so I quickly dashed out of the door, jumped on my bike and raced back home. I'm pretty sure that was the fastest I have ever peddled a bike in my life. When I got home I jumped off my bike and ran downstairs to the basement where Travis, Darren, Scott, and my brothers were playing Super Mario Bros and Paperboy on the Nintendo. They looked over at me and with a smirk on my face I opened my coat and started pulling out the candy I had just stolen and the room went crazy with laughter, excitement, cheers, and a round of high fives. Travis said "well you proved me wrong, you're not a wussy after all kid". At the time I felt like I was on top of the world and when my friend Carter came back he told me he was scared out of his mind. He saw the candy on the table and his eyes got huge and he said "you really went through with it, well I get half because I got the clerk to go outside". It seemed like a fair deal to me so I let Carter take half of it home.

To be honest I felt bad about taking the candy without paying for it so I offered to do chores around the house to earn money because at the time I wanted to save up and go pay for the candy I had stolen. My brother Mark tried to steal candy from the same store a month later but got caught because they just added new cameras, probably because of all the candy I stole from the store. The police arrived at my house with my brother in the back seat, handcuffed, they came up to the house and knocked on the door. I answered the door and the police officer asked if my parents were home, I almost confessed right then and there about stealing the candy, but I saw Mark in the back seat of the car and I ran to get my Dad. My Dad came to the front door and he saw my brother and he was instantly pissed off. The cops said they were going to charge him with shoplifting but they immediately recognized my father because he was the Fire Chief of Greeley, and out of respect for my Dad they let my brother off with a warning knowing the punishment he'd receive from my Dad would be worse than any court ordered punishment. My parents made him get a job as a paperboy to earn money in order to buy candy instead of stealing it, and to keep him busy and out of trouble. Mark "supposedly" slipped up and told our parents that I had also stolen from there once and got away with it, that asshole. My Mom gave me "the look", you know that look of disappointment and of course I admitted it, I mean that shit was weighing heavy on my conscience. My Dad threatened to get the belt and I started balling like a baby so instead they grounded me for a month without pay for doing chores during that entire month. I hated the way that felt and I decided I would never steal again.

My brothers had a few minor incidents growing up and I sat back and observed what not to do. My brother Mark and his friend JT took JT's Dads car, a brand new Cadillac, for a drive at night around the neighborhood and needless to say they took out a few mail boxes as they were 12 years old and had no idea how to drive a car. Then they tried to return it back without JT's parents noticing the scratches and dents, but of course they noticed, the car was parked on the lawn and not in the garage where they left it, not to mention the damage to the car, so JT's Dad called my parents. Again my brother was grounded for life and had to pick up an extra paper route to earn enough money to pay them back half of the cost to fix the damages.

My oldest brother Spencer was on his way to a birthday party for his friend and he asked Mom to pull into Walmart because he wanted to go in and get his friend Ricky a cassette tape of NWA and Too Short. Spencer went into the store and put both cassettes in his jacket pocket. As he was walking toward the exit at the front of the store he heard a voice behind him yell "STOP THIEF", and Spencer took off running to the car. He open the passenger side door and jumped in and told our Mom to hurry up and go. She looked at him and asked "what the hell is going on? I'm not going anywhere until you tell me what just happened". Spencer tried to make up a story about some kids trying to beat him up and just then my Mom noticed a guy walking around the parking lot looking under cars, in cars, and she knew he was looking for someone so she got out and asked the security guard what he looking for and he gave the description of Spencer and my Mom said "that sounds like you're describing my son

Spencer, let me get him for you". She opened the passenger side door and grabbed him by the ear and drug him out of the car and walked him back into the store to return the tapes. The Manager was sure my Mom was going to punish Spencer for his actions and she did just that. You see Spencer had just got a brand new motor scooter for Christmas that he loved so dearly, until my parents took it away along with his Walkman, I don't know which one hit him the hardest, the scooter or the music. As kids we listened to all sorts of music because we loved music. In the basement we would listen to Rap music such as; LL Cool J, Heavy D and the Boyz, Salt and Pepa, NWA, and Too Short, and other non-rap artists, such as Phil Collins, Def Leppard, Poison, AC/DC, Tiffany, Debbie Gibson, Willie Nelson, and George Strait. Quite the assortment.

We weren't always causing trouble in the neighborhood, we raced BMX bikes and our Dad was the medic at the race track. He had his fair share of injuries at the track that he took care of on the spot with his med kit. I was actually really good at racing and ended up going to the State Championships in

Colorado Springs. My parents were so proud of me for winning that they bought me a new bike and I ended up getting hurt during warm ups as I wasn't use to how lite the bike was. I pulled back too hard on the table top jump and the bike flew out from underneath me and I went down on my back and slid on the gravel for 60 feet with no gear on which shredded my back. Thank god my Dad was there and he quickly bandaged up my back before the race began. I qualified in the first race, took first in the second round, and then took first place again in the final round and I brought home the State Championship Trophy. My family was so proud of me and my brother Mark patted me on the back and I started crying because of the pain, he said he forgot and apologized. We all became closer as we grew older and we'd take road trips to go camping in the mountains and see different places in Colorado. One year, during Halloween, we created a haunted house in the basement and charged an entry fee of $5. Surprisingly we ended up making $385 which we donated to the Red Cross, although we almost gave a bunch of kids carbon monoxide poisoning as Mark wanted to be the Chainsaw

Massacre in the Haunted House as we had a chainsaw with no blades on it, but when he cranked it up the fumes almost made everyone sick. My Dad stepped in just in time to shut that down before anyone got hurt, but it scared the living crap out of the kids who went through the haunted house.

Greeley was a great place to be a kid and as we got older we moved a few times because our Dad became the Fire Chief of Black Forest near Colorado Springs and a few years later we moved to Longmont Colorado. Dad retired from being a Fire Chief and became a Bus Driver for the city and Mom became the Accountant and HR Manager for a Micro-Brewery. Needless to say I became very popular at school that year as I became the go to guy for beer. My middle brother Mark moved back to Greeley to attend the fire academy and later he took a contract job to teach Fire Fighting in Iraq during the war. My oldest brother Spencer had moved to Denver after he graduated high school in Colorado Springs and got a job at a sporting goods store and a year later became the Store Manager. It was great because we use to get free snowboard rentals and we would demo all of the new gear sent to the store from companies like Burton or Solomon. It was a great reason to go skiing or snowboarding at Vail, Copper Mountain or Breckenridge. Spencer also joined a multi-level marketing business and asked me if I wanted to join him in making millions. I was 17 at the time and of course I wanted to be a millionaire, but it was very hard for me to find people who would listen to a 17 year old about multi-level marketing, even though I was very professional because I had business cards, hundreds of them. It wasn't all that bad as I enjoyed listening to the tapes, reading motivational books, and traveling to conferences mostly located in the mid-west. I even met a cute girl in Omaha and I wished I'd lived in Omaha so I could date her. I believe that's what sparked my interest in business and I was able to sponsor a few people as well, mostly my friends, and I never made any money from it. After a while I decided not to renew my business and I gave up on it but it got me thinking about the future, my hopes and dreams. Let's just say I owned a lot of Rob Report magazines, listened to "I wanna be rich" by Calloway and wanted to own a mansion, a Lamborghini, a yacht, and a jet.

I graduated from Niwot High School and had no aspirations to go to college because my goal was to start working as soon as possible, you know join the "real world". Spencer told me about a company down the road from his apartment in Denver and he said they were hiring. He thought because I had taken accounting in high school and got straight A's, that it was a perfect for me and I should apply at Charles, Edmund, and Smith (CES Brokerage Firm, also known as a Broker Dealer) as they, in his words, "deal with accounting for stocks and stuff". That night I went online and applied for the Records Clerk position.

Chapter 2 – You're hired

A week after I applied for the job I was at the brewery helping my Mom in the tap room serving beers to the local crowd when I received a call from Human Resources at CES, they asked me to come in for an interview. My parents immediately took me shopping for my first real suit. A few days later I drove down to Denver dressed in my brand new suit and I was extremely nervous the entire drive. I made my way to the CES Headquarters and pulled into the parking lot. I grabbed my black Franklin Planner, got out of the car, and I straightened my tie as I walked into CES. It was a warm summer day and I was sweating profusely, so I went directly into the bathroom to grab a paper towel to wipe the sweat off my forehead. When I came out of the bathroom I checked in with the guard at the desk, still nervous, I waited in the lobby for what felt like a lifetime, but it was only a few minutes. I noticed this guy came out from behind a secured door and introduced himself to me as Doug, the Manager of the Record Center.

I stood up and shook his hand with a firm handshake, I wanted to make a good first impression as my Dad said "Always make a good first impression". We went to Doug's office and he sat down at his desk, he asked if I would close the door, which I did, then I sat in the chair across from him. I reached into my Franklin Planner, pulled out two resumes and I handed him a copy and kept one for myself. Doug began the interview, and not to brag, I provided great answers and strong examples. I was hoping he was impressed with my ability to provide a quick and intelligent response. I tried to refer back to my classes and a few of my personal life experiences, or what little experience I've had at this point in my life. Aside from my ability to overcome difficult situations such as the incident that occurred on the 4th of July when I had my shorts around my ankles.

We finished the interview and Doug asked me when I could start. I thought to myself, should I be excited because it sounds like he's offering me the job and really wants to know for planning purposes. I told him I would have to move to Denver as I currently live in Longmont, but I could start in two weeks and then Doug reached out his hand to shake my hand and he said "You're Hired". He told me I would receive a packet in the mail from Human Resources that contains my salary and benefits information, along with all of the forms that I would have to fill out and bring with me on my first day. I was so excited I told him I looked forward to working with him and his team and I shook his hand again while thanking him for the opportunity. As I walked out to my car, a 1986 Chevy Celebrity POS, POS stands for piece of shit, I was actually overfilled with excitement but also felt a sense of sadness at that very moment because all the sudden it felt real and I knew this was really happening, soon I'd be moving out of my parent's house and officially on my own.

After I left CES, I called Spencer to see if he was home and he said he didn't have to work that day and I should come over. I drove to Spencer's apartment which wasn't a far drive at all from CES, it was just two blocks away. Filled with excitement and joy, I ran into the apartment and told Spencer that I was offered the job right on the spot. My brother smiled and gave me a hug and said "I'm proud of you little bro, you're staying here until you can save up for your own place", I mean how could I say no to that. My brother offered to take me to a restaurant called Sizzler to celebrate. At the same time we both started chanting, "We goin Sizzler, we goin Sizzler". After lunch at Sizzler, I jumped in my POS car and got on I-25 north and headed back to Longmont to share the news with my parents.

I arrived back in Longmont in just under two hours and both of my parents were still at work. Of course I had to call my two best friends, Ryan and Tyler, to tell them the good news. Both Ryan and Tyler came over to the house to hang out, and both were excited for me. I was equally happy for them as they got into the college of their choice, Ryan got accepted to the University of Northern Colorado and Tyler planned to go to BYU or as he called it YBU. Tyler was Mormon but was conflicted and felt everyone who went to BYU were clones of one another and had no individuality, hence YBU. He changed his mind and decided to go to the University of Northern Colorado, the same college as Ryan.

When my parents got home I was frowning as if I had bad news. My dad looked at me and said "it's alright son, you'll get the next one" and I looked up at him, then in my saddest voice I said "but there won't be a next one" and I started to smile, "because I got the job and I start in two weeks". My dad smiled and called me a rascal and my mom had tears swelling in her eyes and she began to cry. She said they were tears of joy but we both knew she was sad because I was the last of the boys to leave the house and now they'll be "empty nesters". I hugged my mom and said "don't worry mom, I won't be that far away and I'll be living with Spencer until I can save up to get my own place. Plus I'll make sure to come back and do some laundry and have you make me my favorite meal, Kraut Burgers". My mom smiled and said "I'm very proud of you, this is big, let's go to the brewery to celebrate".

At the time I was only 18 but I've had a few beers over the past few years, mostly supervised by my parents. On occasion I would help my mom serve beers at festivals like the Great American Beer Fest or Brew at the Zoo. I was very outgoing and loved chatting with people to get to know them. Plus I got hit on by older women who wanted me to top off their glass if they gave me a kiss on the cheek, so my Mom had me "work the crowd" as she would call it. I was friends with a lot of people but my closest friends were Ryan and Tyler who were the kind of friends that would stick by you through good and bad times and I was always there to help them in their times of need.

The day came for me to pack my things, mostly clothes, since I didn't own any furniture and move down to Denver. Spencer told me he had a futon I could sleep on and he had a small coat closet for my clothes, so I loaded up my POS car and gave my parents one last hug and kiss goodbye. Again my Mom started crying which made me tear up as I got in my car and drove off, ready to officially join the "real world" starting at 8:00 am Monday morning.

Chapter 3 – Making connections

The weekend flew by as I got situated at Spencer's place, unpacking all of my clothes into the coat closet, which took a whole 45 minutes, and then we went grocery shopping as Mom and Dad gave me $300 for food and gas. I bought the basics; ramen noodles, water, peanut butter, jelly, and bread. After grocery shopping my brother and I went to Clement Park and skated around the lake at the park on our rollerblades. We took off the rollerblades and threw the football around for a few hours until the sun began to set. It was a beautiful view as the sun went down behind the mountains in the west and the sky lit up in a glow. We headed back to the apartment and I quickly ran an iron over my clothes after I ate some delicious ramen noodles. My brother and I played a few rounds of Super Mario Bros on the Nintendo until 11:00 pm and then we decided to call it a night. The futon was actually pretty comfortable and I slept well that night.

Monday morning arrived in the blink of an eye. I woke up at 7:00 am to allow myself time to brush my teeth, get dressed, and drive to work. I arrived at 7:50 AM, 10 minutes early, and checked in at the front desk. Cheryl from HR came out to greet me and we headed back to her office to get my id badge. I opened my Franklin Planner and gave her all the forms I had to fill out from the packet. She pulled out a few forms from her desk and handed them to me, the first one was a letter welcoming me to the CES Team and stated my salary was $14,000 annually and the second form covered all the benefits, 401K, health, dental, vision, and so on. Cheryl walked me to an office down the hall from hers and told me to sit behind the computer and login as she handed me a form with a login id. She instructed me to complete a few mandatory training courses and after that she would come back and get me. When I finished the courses I notified Cheryl and she walked me down to the Record Center to Doug's office. Doug shook my hand and welcomed me to the team. We walked over to an employee and Doug said "this is Charles, you'll be training with him". I shook Charles hand and sat down, I took the pen and paper Doug gave me and started taking copious amounts of notes as Charles quickly walked me through the process of imaging forms that are received from the various departments at CES and then putting them into a box to archive the documents at an offsite storage facility. Charles also told me that part of my job is to drive a minivan over to the Teller Building at nine, twelve, three, and five, to pick up boxes of documents, load them into the minivan, and drive back to the Wadsworth building to have them imaged and archived.

I trained with Charles for a week and I quickly got the hang of the job. It was summer and I had to wear a dress shirt, tie, slacks and dress shoes which sucked as I sweated a lot and went through dress shirts quickly, plus Charles was a bit of jerk to work with but I really enjoyed my daily interactions with the various people in each department as I made my rounds to pick up boxes of documents to have imaged and archived. I would flirt a little bit with a girl named Lisa in Financial Planning and she flirted back, she was a bit older than me, not by much, probably in her early twenties. She had gorgeous red hair and beautiful green eyes but I thought there was no way she'd ever give me the time of day, so

I stayed focused on my job and hoped to get promoted to New Accounts in a year or two.

Almost a full year into the job I became close friends with Marcus, this guy who worked in the Teller building mailroom and was really nice and chill. We hung out on weekends and played basketball at Clement Park or went to house parties near DU (Denver University). Marcus grew up in Five Points and lived at home with his Mom, but he'd crash at our place as often as possible. Marcus told me there was a lot crime in Five Points and he needed to get out of there as quickly as possible. At that point, I had saved enough money to get my own place so I asked Marcus if he wanted to become roommates and go half on an apartment. Marcus looked at me and said are you serious. I shook my head yes and he accepted by shaking my hand and giving me a hug. I pulled out an apartment finder magazine and we started flipping through it and found a few places in our price range, so we hopped in my car and went looking for an apartment.

Marcus got a few leasing agents phones numbers and we also found an apartment, a two bed two bath, for the right price off of South Quebec Street and Mineral Drive. It was a bit further away from work than my brother's place, but the timing was perfect because he started dating someone and needed his space, if you catch my drift. I signed the lease on my own and we moved in to the new apartment that weekend. Needless to say we turned the place into the ultimate bachelor pad with bean bag chairs, cheap artwork that I found by the dumpster in the apartment complex, and a cheap couch that we bought from a friend of a friend, good thing Marcus had a truck. It worked out well as we'd carpool to and from work and when I turned 21, Marcus took me to my first strip club downtown called the Diamond Cabaret.

Doug hired Marcus in our department and he had me train him on my job functions as I was promoted to a New Accounts Specialist position. With my raise I was able to buy a used Honda Accord as my POS (piece of shit) Chevy Celebrity was no longer a celebrity and stopped running three months ago. I was so grateful that Marcus was there to drive me to and from work that I offered to pay for gas, bought groceries, and I bought Marcus drinks at the clubs. Coming from entirely different worlds, we were able to see past that and became great friends, I had his back and Marcus had mine.

I was promoted again a year and a half later to a position in Customer Accounting where I approved transactions, such as; checks, fed fund wires, and journal entries, as long as the client sold enough securities or had sufficient cash available in their account to cover the transaction. This was right up my alley as I loved learning about the stock market and the process of moving funds from one account to another. A few months into the job Marcus came to me and told me his mother was ill, Cancer, and he'd have to move back in with her which I completely understood and at this point I was making enough to support the cost of the apartment on my own, but I was definitely sad about the news of Marcus' mom and to have my good friend move out. Marcus and I kept in touch but unfortunately he eventually lost his job because he kept missing work in order to take his mother to get chemo treatments. I tried to give him as much money as I could to help him out with medical expenses, food, rent, but I felt it wasn't enough. I called as often as I could and eventually Marcus stopped answering my calls. I had never been to his Mom's house otherwise I would have drove over there to make sure everything was ok but I feared it wasn't. I stopped sending money as Marcus never returned my calls, and it broke my heart but we parted ways and we've never spoken to one another since.

Shortly after Marcus had moved out, I received a call from my longtime friend Ryan who graduated from UNC and was looking for a job. He asked me if CES was hiring and I told him there were a lot of jobs available so I submitted his resume for a position in Broker Transfer. Ryan interviewed and was offered the job the following week and I received a referral bonus of $1,000. He moved down to Denver and since I had the extra room Ryan moved in with me. Honestly I was happy to have one of my best friends living with me and working at the same company, but I also thought about Marcus often and hoped he and his Mom were ok.

Shortly after Ryan started, my brother Spencer asked if there were any opening in my department for Managers as he'd been running the sporting goods store for several years now. I knew there was an opening for an Assistant Supervisor job on one of the teams so I submitted the referral for the job and Spencer was offered a Customer Accounting Specialist position as they hired internally for the Assistant Supervisor job. Again I received another $1,000 bonus and I was so happy to have my brother and my best friend working at CES with me.

My apartment lease was about to expire and CES had moved their campus to southeast Denver near the DTC (Denver Tech Center) which happened to be close to where I already lived with Ryan, but it was further for Spencer so all three of us agreed to get an apartment together at Palomino Park which had a lot of great amenities and was only five minutes away from work. We were able to get a 3 bedroom, 2 bath, and the best part was the bar at the clubhouse. They had happy hour every Friday from 4 – 7 and there were a lot of young professionals that lived there. Spencer broke up with his girlfriend and the three of us were all single so we had fun seeing each other "try" to meet woman at bars and clubs. We all went on a few dates here and there but nothing ever got serious.

Spencer having past managerial experience moved up quickly in the company and became the Customer Accounting Supervisor for the Northeast Team and I worked on the Southeast Team under Lauren. Lauren was by far the best boss I'd ever worked for, even better than Doug. She was very hands on, explained things in great detail which I soaked up like a sponge. She even played a joke on me and said I accidentally approved a Fed Fund Wire for $5 Million and sent the funds to the wrong account. The look on my face must have been priceless because she couldn't keep it in and started busting up laughing. I was relieved it was only a joke but I'm pretty sure I shit my pants for a minute there.

Lauren hired someone new on the team who was close to my age named Todd. He sat with me and I trained him on the procedures and processes involved with being a Customer Accounting representative. Todd was able to learn the job just as fast as I did, he was smart and I was impressed. After training and once he was on his own, we hung out after work and became friends. I thought Todd's parents must have a lot of money because he drove a BMW M3 and had a Ducati motorcycle. He had his own apartment which was decked out with lavish furniture so he must have rich parents. I never asked him how he could afford all of it until one day he asked me to take a box to a friend of his who lived in Parker which is southeast of Denver, he said he couldn't do it because he had to visit his parents that afternoon. He gave me the address and of course being the good friend that I am, I drove it over there but the address was for a Mexican restaurant, so I called Todd and asked if I had the right address and he asked me if I saw a red car which just happened to pull up. Todd said give them the package and they'll give you an envelope and just come back here and we'll grab a bite to eat before I go over to my parents' house. I got out of the car and the other guy got out of his car and said "are you Todd's friend?", thinking to myself what the hell is going on I nodded and walked over and handed him the package and he handed me an envelope. He turned around, got back in his car and drove off.

I got back in my car and immediately called Todd, I asked if he just had me do a deal with that guy, knowing not to say drug deal on the phone. Todd said he couldn't tell me what he had me doing because he knew I'd never agree to it, and he was right about that. As I drove back to Todd's place I was pissed off thinking how could he do that to me and what if that guy was a cop, I could have been arrested. When I got to his place I walked in, furious, and I threw the envelop full of cash on the table and I told Todd to never put me in that position again. I felt as though Todd had used our friendship, my trust for his own personal gain and protection. Todd reached into the envelope and gave me $300 and said "I'm sorry, I'll never do that to you again. I just haven't dealt with that guy before so I wasn't 100% sure of the deal, so yes, I was covering my own ass. I know this doesn't make up for it but I am sorry!"

After that Todd and I remained friends but I was always careful and cautious about where we went and who he was around because Todd had other friends he ran with who I assumed also sold drugs. I was curious about why Todd sold drugs so I asked him about his upbringing and what led him to become a dealer. He said he was raised in a normal family, just wanted to do it for the money. He said he went to a few high school parties back in the day and sold ecstasy. Todd said he started making good money so he upped his game to other drugs and started getting a variety of clients. It just so happens that Todd's sister, Heather, was an assistant for a Managing Director at CES and during those infamous Christmas parties she would connect him with a lot of clients for his business, Director's, Vice Presidents, and Senior VP's. Now I knew how Todd got a job at CES, because his sister got him the job as no one wanted their dirty little secret out there. Todd made me swear on my life that I would never say anything and I agreed, and then he told me some of the names of his clients at CES. Needless to say I was shocked as many of them had families and seemed fairly normal. I had been with CES for 6 years now, so I knew every single one of them and I definitely looked at them differently from that day forward. Todd said "hey man, it's not what you know, it's who you know". I said "more like who you sell weed and blow to".

Chapter 4 – The exam

I had my monthly one on one with Lauren and I told her I felt I had learned everything I could about the job, that I was ready to start studying for the series 7 exam as I wanted to become a Financial Advisor. She said CES offered a class but you have to study first and get a 70% on the pre-test before they even send you to the class downtown.

I ordered my books and when they arrived I started studying day and night. I even convinced Ryan to study with me so we could take the test at the same time. We spent every night after work and weekends studying for the exam. The material was as dry as the desert and some parts were pretty complex, especially options. Well, they were tough for me but Ryan seemed to understand them right away, smart ass. He eventually became my tutor because he said he learned study habits in college and would teach them to me, since I never went to college.

We put together flash cards and would quiz each other. Ryan still seemed to grasp the material better than I did, he said it's because he took finance and economics in college, again, smart ass. He took the pre-test and got an 85% on it and started taking the course downtown. I took it and scored a 54%, so clearly I needed to study some more. Todd decided to study at that time and he paid for an online program which gave you practice tests just like the ones on the exam. Leave it up to the drug dealer to find a program "just like the exam" although he paid a pretty penny for it, $850. He and I took the online exams over the course of a month and we both scored above an 80% so we decided to take the pre-test and both passed, he got a 73% and I got a 79%.

Just as Todd and I got into the next class, Ryan finished and took the exam and passed it with a score of 87%. As my manager Lauren said he studied way too hard as you just need a 70% to pass, but I don't think Ryan knew any other way as he always scored high on tests. He said it was just all memorization, a skill he learned in college. Ryan said he would cram for a test the night before and because it was so fresh in his mind he would get passing scores on them, or at least he said that was the method to his madness. I think with my high level of stress that method probably wouldn't work for me. I took Ryan out that night to celebrate him passing the exam which was a bad idea to party that hard when we had to go to work the next day. I woke up and went to work even though I fought a hangover at work and pounded waters and Gatorade like there was no tomorrow, horrible idea to go that hard on a school night but we had a blast.

Todd and I attend the class downtown every night for a month and we were scoring lower on the practice tests than the ones we took online, but we still felt confident about being able to pass the test. The instructor told us to schedule the exam right after the class as he had a higher pass rate, better retention of information, I guess Ryan was right about his technique. The instructor did a much better job of explaining options than the book or even the online program ever could. Having a visual helped as the instructor told us to get out a piece of paper and make a large square with nine blocks inside. He called this the Option Chart and said the first thing we do when we sit down to take the test is draw this chart on the piece of paper they give us to use.

He told us the exam has a large bank of questions and there are roughly 50 questions on options, approximately 35 of them deal with options strategies and the remaining 15 questions are on option markets, rules, and suitability. He said because most of the questions focus on options strategies, that's why he focused on that during class. It became pretty straight forward after a few examples, if you buy a call, you want a bull market and the stock to go up and if you buy a put option you want a bear market and the stock price to go down, and vice versa if you sell a call or put. It got a lot more complicated with straddles, spreads, and complex option strategies like condors, iron condors, butterfly spreads, box spreads, and the list goes on and on. I thought the course was great as I learned a lot, I mean a lot.

Todd and I filled out the U4 form and scheduled a date to take the exam. We kept studying every day until the day came for us to take the exam. CES gives you a free vacation day, if you pass, but if you don't pass they dock you a sick day. Both Todd and I showed up early at the location to take the test and we walked in, registered, and put all of our belongings in a locker. We each got assigned a computer and they give us headphones to block out noise, a pencil, paper, a calculator and we had 6 hours to answer 250 questions. The lady running the testing facility said "you have to get a 70% or better to pass, good luck, and begin".

Right away I did brain dump of all the information I could retain from the various courses I took and all the books I read onto the piece of paper she gave me. I created my option chart, and wrote other notes down regarding rules and regulations, the act of 33 and 34, retirement plan information I learned from the publication 590 about mandatory distributions at the age of 70 and a half, Qualified plans versus Non-Qualified, etc. That took me 20 minutes to get everything on paper and then I started the computer based exam. The online program Todd and I took said it helps to take test online to get use to the structure of the exam and it definitely helped as the format was similar. I was feeling pretty good in the beginning about my answers and I completed the first half in an hour and 45 minutes, which seemed fast. Then I had to take a mandatory hour lunch and came back to take the second half. The second set of questions were a lot harder than the first set and when I finished the test and clicked submit, the computer read "Are you sure you want to submit as all results are final", my nerves kicked in and my hand started shaking. I clicked submit and waited for what felt like a lifetime but was 10 seconds and my results popped up on the screen, I got 174 questions correct which means I scored a 69%. I fucking missed it by one question, I was furious and just wanted to pick up the computer and throw it out the window. I felt my face turn red and my eyes began to fill with tears, so I got up and walked to the lobby where the lady behind the desk printed out my form and didn't say a word to me as she saw the expression and anger on my face. I gathered my belongings out of the locker and left.

Todd called and asked where I was and how I did on the test, I told him I was at the bar by the house getting shit faced because I failed the test by one question. He said he was on his way and I asked how he did and he said he passed with a 74%. I felt like such a loser because now I had two friends who both passed the series 7 exam and I failed it. The good thing about Todd, being a true salesman, when he arrived at the bar he cheered me up by telling me how smart I was and how close I got, that I shouldn't give up and he and sold me on retaking the exam. We stayed at the bar and celebrated Todd passing the 7 and ended up meeting a few older women who lived in Highlands Ranch. We continued the party at one of their houses and she kept bringing up how she was recently divorced. Todd and her friend disappeared into one bedroom and she grabbed my hand and took me upstairs to her room. I was drunk and she said she just wanted sex, nothing more, plus I had to leave right after as her kids come back from their Grandparent's house in the morning. She took off my clothes and laid me on the bed, then she took off her clothes and that was my first and only one night stand. I woke up at home the next day, not remembering how I got home and I couldn't remember her name. I called Todd and he said he took care of me and asked if I had a good time, which I did. But I was also freaking out about getting an STD so I called the doctor and made an appointment to get tested the very next day. I went to the Doctor and they ran tests and everything came back clean, thank god. Now I could go back to focusing on work and studying, again, for the series 7.

While studying the first time around I had applied for an Assistant Supervisor Position on the Retirement Plan Services team, Lauren put a good word in for me with the Supervisor, Dave, and he offered me the job. I told him I planned to start studying again and would take the exam in 90 days, hopefully for the last time. After a month went by I took the pre-test and passed and scheduled my exam on the 90 day mark. They asked if I wanted to take the course again downtown and I took them up on it. All by myself this time, I went to the class every day for a month, but this time I saw a familiar face in the class. It was Lisa who still worked in Financial Planning, but she said she wanted to become a Financial Advisor as well someday. She told me she was on a track to get all of her licenses, the series 7 which is the general securities representative exam and the series 66 is a combination of the 63 and 65 which allows you to give advice and guidance and then she planned to take the CFP (Certified Financial Planner) exam. I told her I was impressed and I would be happy to help her get there. She smiled and said "ok you can take the tests for me". I told her I would if I could.

Lisa and I studied together at the library and she thought I was super smart as I knew so much about the industry and the exam already. She said "wow, somebody did their homework. You sure do know a lot about the test" and I just shrugged and smiled but I didn't tell her I had already taken the exam and failed. I invited her over to my place one weekend to study and we started taking about options and margin requirements. We were both flirting again just as we did a long time ago and we both laughed when we came to the part about straddles, spreads, and naked calls and puts. Sitting side by side her hand touched mine and she looked into my eyes and smiled, I smiled back and she leaned in, pressed her lips together and closing her eyes. I couldn't believe this was really happening, I leaned in as well and our lips connected in a passionate kiss. We got up, kept kissing, and went to my room where articles of clothing started flying off our bodies onto the floor. Before I knew it we were in my bed making love to one another, kissing and caressing each other. Lisa was so beautiful with her red hair and green eyes, I couldn't stop looking deep into those amazing green eyes. My heart melted as I focused on her moans and facial expressions. We made love over and over for several hours. As I laid there next to her I thought how great it felt to be with her and let's be honest, it had been a long time since I had dated anyone. I had the occasional date here and there, not to mention that one night stand, but with Lisa I could see a future together. We both wanted similar things out of life and we had an obvious attraction to one another, so I decided why not, I asked if she wanted to date and she smiled and said "you mean go steady" and we both laughed.

Another month went by and Lisa and I continued to study together, with the occasional hookup to relieve stress, until the day came when I had to take the exam. I decided to take the exam on a Friday in case I didn't pass again, then I wouldn't have to face anyone at work the next day and could have the weekend to recover. I started getting nervous again as I checked in. I sat down, did my brain dump again on the piece of paper and started taking the test but this time all of the questions seemed easy and I felt more confident about my answers when I pressed the submit button to get my results. I nervously awaited my fate and the screen popped up with a score of 73% and I almost jumped out of my seat. I was so excited that I had finally passed the exam that I jumped up and quickly gathered my belongings out of the locker and the lady behind the counter smiled at me and said "I remember you. Great job, I knew you could do it, congratulations". I grabbed my sheet of paper that said I passed the exam and I immediately called Lisa at work. She told me congratulations and said she was so proud of me. She offered to take me out that night after work to celebrate. I proceeded to call everyone else, Mom, Dad, Mark, Spencer, Tyler, Ryan, and Todd, I even tried to call Marcus but he never answered. Spencer and Ryan said we would celebrate on Saturday as they knew Lisa and I had plans to celebrate later that night. When Lisa got off work she came over and we went out for dinner to a nice restaurant in the LoDo

(Lower Downtown) area. Lisa reached across the table and grabbed my hand and looked me in the eyes and said "I love you". I said "I love you too" and she tried to be romantic and rub her foot on my crotch but she came in hard and fast and kicked me in the balls. After a bit of laughter and crying on my part, we enjoyed the rest of our dinner and went back to my place. While I drove us home she whispered in my ear that she would make me fell all better. We got back to my place and went inside, Lisa grabbed my hand and walked me to my bedroom were we made love again, but this time we didn't use protection. It was one of the best days of my life as I felt a deep connection to her.

Lisa took the series 7 exam but she didn't pass it her first time either. Unfortunately, the very next day the Chief Operating Officer (COO) held a town hall meeting in the cafeteria and she announced CES will be closing the Denver Headquarters and relocating their operations to New Jersey and Florida based on the functions of each department. Because I worked in Retirement Planning my job and department was planning to move to Florida. Customer Accounting and Broker

Transfer were both relocating to New Jersey so Spencer and Ryan opted to take the severance package. Ryan was able to quickly find a job with a competitor and my brother Spencer decided to go back to school and get a degree in computer science. Todd ended up moving to New Jersey with Customer Accounting and became the department trainer and later was promoted to Vice President of the department. I'm pretty sure most of his clients also moved to New Jersey so he still has some additional cash flow.

Lisa's department was planning to move to New Jersey and we met for lunch one day to discuss what we both wanted to do. She was still upset about not passing the exam and said she was mad at me for not being more supportive about that, although I thought I had been supportive. She was even more upset at me for not immediately offering to move with her to New Jersey. I told her I was trying to think of all possible solutions but I wasn't aware I had a timeline to decide. We had only been dating for a few months but it felt like years had passed and we were an old married couple, arguing about stupid shit. I told her that if we love each other we could make it work, but I guess she felt differently because she told me she didn't love me and wanted to break up as we were both headed in different directions. She broke up with me on the spot and said she was saving us both the heartache. I tried to talk her out of it because I thought she really loved me but she said "no, it's just best for the both of us", she got in her car and drove off in tears. A few days had passed and I tried to call her every day before I left Colorado but she never picked up the phone. Heartbroken, I packed my things into the truck and I hit the road, on my way to Florida the Sunshine State.

Chapter 5 – Hard Times

After a long drive, and by long I mean several days on the road, I arrived in Jacksonville Florida. I pulled the truck into my new apartment complex off of Southside Boulevard near a mall. I had never traveled to the east coast before and I definitely wasn't ready for the heat and humidity as I stepped out of the truck at the leasing office to sign my paperwork and pick up my keys. I was also taken back by all the palm trees and vegetation. Florida was a lot greener than I had thought, I guess I thought it was all sand and beaches.

I walked into the leasing office and paid my deposit, first and last month's rent and took the truck to my building to unload it. I got an apartment on the ground floor and thought I could unload everything by myself but that wasn't the case. I asked a couple of guys in the neighborhood for their help and offered to pay them to unload my coach, bed, furniture and boxes. They agreed to help and I paid them $100 each.

With all of my furniture in the apartment, I dropped the truck off and went to explore a bit. I drove my Honda to Jacksonville Beach, then headed north to Neptune Beach and Atlantic Beach. I parked my car and walked a few steps to the beach. I couldn't believe I was staring out at the Atlantic Ocean. I thought to myself, this boy from Colorado has come a long way.

I decided to take a stroll down the beach and began to think a lot about Lisa and what I did wrong, wondering how I could have made things better, but it made me mad just thinking about it because I felt hopeless and alone. She could have moved out here with me and we'd be together, but no, she was selfish and didn't give a shit about me. After walking south on the beach for an hour and getting myself worked up, I stopped and sat on the beach for a bit, I began to calm down after looking out at the ocean and listening to the sound of waves crashing on the shore. Seeing the vastness of the ocean made me feel small, it made my problems feel small and silly. I got up, brushed myself off and decided to head back north to Atlantic Beach where I stepped into a bar for a bit to have a beer. I didn't stay out long as I had a lot of unpacking to do so I headed back to my apartment, but not without making a few wrong turns. I no longer had the mountains to base my sense of direction off of and I didn't have a compass in my car.

I stayed up until 3 am unpacking all of my boxes and got up at 10 am the next day and started putting things away. I spent all day organizing and getting my place set up, at this point in my life I was a pro at it because of all the times I had moved before. I went to bed early as I started work the next day at my new office. Monday morning arrived and I headed into work, stopping by the coffee shop next to the office to get my morning cup of coffee, ok let's be honest, it was a Venti Triple Carmel Macchiato Skinny, because I'm obviously watching my weight.

I pulled into the parking lot of CES and they had a giant statue of a Bull and a Bear going head to head right next to the main entrance. It was the first day of reporting to the new office for all of us but I noticed several of my team members were waiting in the lobby next to someone holding a sign that read RPS for Retirement Plan Services. I walked up and introduced myself, the person holding the sign said "Hi, I'm Rob and I'll take you all upstairs to the department once everyone has arrived". I looked at my team and said "I think we're all here".

We all settled into the new building and shockingly my boss Dave changed his mind at the last minute and decided not to move, so his boss Jim said there was an opening for a Supervisor position and he mentioned they were considering me for the job. I applied for it and a week later they offered me the job. I transitioned into the role and my team was happy for me, they even said I did a better job of managing the team than Dave as I had regular one on ones and really focused on developing my employees to get them to where they wanted to go in the company. Shortly after I moved to Florida I started taking college courses to get my degree in Finance from an accredited university. Over the next few months I also studied for the Series 6, 65, and 66. I planned to take my CFP (Certified Financial Planner Exam) after I got my degree as my goal was to eventually become a Financial Advisor. I heard the CFP was tough as it's a seven hour exam, broken into two 3 hour chunks with a 40 minute lunch and the test costs $695.

Some time went by and I tried to reach out to Lisa but she never answered. I was getting lonely living in Florida all by myself so I created an online profile on a dating website. The first date I had was with a woman named Kim, we meet at a restaurant close to the mall and Kim was from Guangzhou China and didn't speak a word of English, so needless to say it was a very interesting date. For my next date I met Stacey, she was a waitress at Hooters and she asked me what kind of car I drove right when we sat down. When I told her I drove a Honda Accord, she got up and walked out on me. I went on a few more dates after that but I never made the same connection I had with Lisa. To keep my mind off of her I kept studying and focused on the exams. I would get off work and go to the library to study, I would stay there from 5 – 8 ever night for a month and scheduled the exams. I took the 6, 65, and 66 all in the same week and passed them with flying colors. I must be getting better at this studying thing, I guess Ryan was right, college teaches you study skills and memorization tactics.

After living in Florida for almost a full year, I received a call from Lisa, just out of the blue. I answered my cell phone and sounded surprised, because I was. I thought I would never hear from her again. When she spoke she said "hey" which sounded very somber, I asked if everything was ok and she said she had some news for me and thought I should sit down if I wasn't already. I said "I am sitting down, why what's wrong". Lisa told me she found out she was pregnant right after we broke up, I interrupted and said "when you broke up with me" and she continued by saying I was the father of her daughter, a little girl named Sara. I was in shock and didn't say a word. She told me that when she found out she was pregnant she had to move back in with her parents to take care of Sara because she couldn't afford everything on her own. She said "I thought about calling you but I was so upset that you moved away I decided I could do this all on my own and I didn't need you, but now I need your help, financially". Then she told me she had no choice but to file for child support, still in shock and not saying a word, I began to feel emotions of anger and heartbreak again, on the verge of tears I said "how dare you keep this from me! And you tell me now, why because you just want child support, not because you thought I should know that I'm the father of Sara, but just because you're selfish and need money" and I abruptly hung up the phone. It felt like my whole body was shaking as I looked down at my hands, they were trembling, I felt the wetness of my tears roll down my cheek. I sat there, mind racing, wondering why she would do that to me, why was she so mad that I moved away when she was the one who decided to end it all without consideration to move with me to Florida. I started crying and so filled with rage wondering what I did for her to hate me so much.

I told myself I would call her back after I calmed down a bit and could think clearly. I even tried to put myself in her shoes as to why she waited so long to call me and tell me, but the thought process didn't make sense to me. My mind tried to come up with every possible scenario like maybe she met someone else and told him he was the father and he made her get a test and since it came back not his, he dumped her, so now she's in a hard spot and needs money or maybe she thought I abandoned her and she wrote me off until she needed the money, I don't know. I tried not to think about it, but it was all I could think about. I told myself if I keep thinking about all the why's that I'd go mad and keep getting more and more upset about it, that I needed to continue my school work and go on with my life the best I could.

I applied for the Financial Advisor Program at CES and was accepted as a candidate because my Manager and my Managing Director gave me rave reviews. They accepted me into the program knowing I was going to school to get my degree in Finance. A week into the program I received a court ordered letter and a kit to take a paternity test, I knew Lisa was serious when I saw that. I filled out the documents and swabbed my cheek and mailed everything back. I called her right after and left a voice message "I filled out the form and submitted the kit. I want to see proof she's my child before I send you a penny". About a month went by and she mailed me the results and Sara was definitely my daughter. In the package there were more forms I had to fill out. Lisa included a photo of Sara which brought me to tears, she was so beautiful and looked so peaceful wrapped in her blanket.

I sent the forms back along with my first check for the month of $400. I called Lisa and told her I would try to send more than just the required amount and she said that would be helpful. I asked her if she'd be willing to move to Florida to give it another try and she said no, she couldn't leave her parents in Colorado. Later she told me the real reason was because she started dating someone and has deep feelings for him. Again, I was heartbroken because she didn't want me and she wanted another guy to raise my daughter. I told her once I had enough money saved up, I'd fly out to see Sara.

Despite everything happening in my life at that moment and falling on hard times, I was able to pass the program and started building my book of clients. I held a few seminars on retirement planning and obtained a few clients from that, but the pay for a beginning Financial Advisor wasn't all that great and I was trying to give Lisa as much money as I could afford, which wasn't very much, and I was cutting back on my spending and stopped eating out and going to parties. I went out for drinks with some friends from work, only because they offered to buy so why not, and one asked me if I knew anyone who smoked weed and where he could get some. I had no idea as I had never done a single drug in my life but if we lived in Colorado I could have hooked him up with Todd, and then it hit me, I could call Todd and see if he has any contacts in Florida for a supplier that I could contact to buy weed from and that way I could make some quick cash by selling weed. I mean hey it worked for Todd so why not and I could use the money, badly.

I called Todd when I got home and he said "who needs a supplier in Florida when you've got FedEx". He asked me what I wanted to sell and I told him I was pretty sure a lot of people smoked weed out here. He said he would get in touch with his guy and get back to me. Just as I studied for my exams I began to research online about all the different drugs out there, slang terms, cost, weight, and jail time for previous dealers. I needed to know exactly what I was getting into if I was really going through with this. I had to be smart about it so I read up on Weed, Marijuana,

Cannabis, since that was going to be the first drug I would sell. I learned the slang terms for measurement first, the gram "dime bag", the "eighth" of an ounce, the "quarter" of an ounce or the "Q", and then there's the "ounce", "O", or "zip" as it was called back in the day. Prices varied from $10 for a dime bag, ok that makes sense, all the way up to $280 or more for an ounce, and if it was top shelf weed I could get more money for it.

Todd called me back and said he spoke to his guy, he told me he actually has a supplier for me in Saint Augustine rather than going through the whole mail process. The guy's name was Chuck and Todd gave me his phone number. He said "when you call him, tell him Carlos calls you Charles", that way he'll know you're good to go and can trust you. I had flash backs to the time I did Todd a favor back in Colorado but this time, I was all in. I said thanks and told him everything that happened with Lisa and why I needed to do this. He told me to keep my head up and be careful when dealing, make connections and develop trust, friends of friends to start with, and keep a low profile.

I took a loan from my 401K, $10,000, and called Chuck. I said "Hi Chuck, I'm friends with Carlos and he said to tell Charles hello. I'd like to meet you and discuss a business proposition with you". Chuck said "Ok cool man, meet me at the dock next to the Bridge of Lions tomorrow at 10:00 am. I'm the last boat on the left". I told him I would see him tomorrow even though it was a work day for me, I decide to take a personal day.

I left Jacksonville at 9:00 am and drove down to Saint Augustine from Jacksonville which took about 30 minutes. I parked on the street next to the fort called Castillo de San Marcos and walked around the town a bit since I got there early and I had never been to Saint Augustine which is sad because it's an amazing city, plus it claims to be the oldest city in the US, lots of history and I love history. Time flew by pretty fast and I found the dock next to the Bridge of Lions. I walked down the dock, feeling anxious and nervous because I was carrying $5,000 in my backpack. I was going to ask Chuck for thirteen "O's", I guessed the price of 13 ounces would cost me around $3,640 if he charged me $280 per ounce. That way I could sell it for $340 an ounce and profit $780. Plus what if I couldn't do this, I didn't want to be out to much money. I came to the last boat on the dock, a 45 Cantius Cruiser Yacht with the name Wet Dream / Saint Augustine, FL on it. It was 10:00 am on the dot and I approached the boat and knocked on the side of it to announce my arrival and the back door swung open. Chuck stepped out and he did not look how I imagined, he was tall and skinny, old white guy with a grey beard and leathery tan skin. He was wearing flip flops, khaki shorts, and a blue Hawaiian shirt with colorful flowers all over it. I thought to myself, is this my supplier or Jimmy Buffett.

Chuck waved me over, said hello, and told me to come aboard. I got on the boat and walked over to Chuck and shook his hand. He welcomed me into the cabin of the boat and then he closed the door. He didn't have security personnel or anything, but he did ask me if I had any weapons on me, I shook my head no. He asked me to lift up my shirt and do a 360, I thought nothing of it and did as he asked, then Chuck said "Ok man you're good, I trust you. So how do you know Carlos? He's the only person that calls me Charles". I told him about Todd and my past experience which I guess Chuck found funny as he laughed at my story of when I did the drop without knowing what I was doing. He said "Classic Todd". I said "you know Todd?" Chuck smiled and said he had no idea who Todd was but it sounded like something a Todd would do. I thought this guy has been out in the sun way to much or he's just messing with me.

Chuck took a liking to me and offered me a drink and asked if I wanted to hit a line with him. I declined and I told him I have never touched a single drug in my life and he laughed at that too. I thought to myself, it's a bit early for a drink, but I guess when you live on a yacht and you dress like Jimmy Buffett then it's 5 o'clock somewhere. He handed me a rum and coke and asked what I wanted to sell, I took a sip of the rum and coke which tasted pretty good and I said weed. He asked me how much I wanted to buy again, so I told him I wanted to start out with 13 ounces. He smiled and said "you know in Florida possession over 20 grams is an indication of intent to distribute, and you want 13 ounces". I thought, oh shit what if he's a cop and he's going to arrest me, I could get up to 5 years in jail and have to pay a fine of $5,000, again I did my homework. I said yes and if everything goes well I plan to buy a lot more, if that's ok.

I thought about Sara and started to get nervous while Chuck walked over to a cabinet and opened a safe. He grabbed a brick of weed and said that should cover it and told me to pay him $3,500 and we'll call it good. I didn't want to insult Chuck and start off on the wrong foot by asking him to weigh it so I took the money out, counted out $3,500 and then tried to hand it to him, but he said "just leave it on the table". I asked Chuck what else he distributes just in case I wanted to expand my business and he told me whatever I want to buy, he's got it.

I stood up, put the weed in my backpack and said "thank you, I'll be in touch". Chuck was already standing and he reached out to shake my hand, he said "pleasure doing business with you and if you're ever in town for fun, just give me a call". He seemed like a really nice guys and I told him I'd call him soon. Just as I was about to walk out the door I heard a noise behind us, I turned around to see a young busty blonde came out of the bedroom, completely naked, she smiled and waved at me then grabbed a bottle of water from the fridge and went back into the bedroom. Chuck patted me on the back like he was pushing me out the door, he smiled and said "I carry the little blue pill too" then winked at me.

I got off the boat and walked faster than I've ever walked back to my car with a backpack full of weed, feeling the same as I did when I was a kid after I stole candy from the corner store, scared I was going to get caught. I got in my car and I couldn't believe that just happened. As I drove back to Jacksonville I remember driving the speed limit the entire way on I-95. I pulled into my apartment complex and turned around and went out the exit because I just remembered something, I need a scale to weigh this stuff. I turned back around again and called myself an idiot because I had the drugs in the car and needed to get it home, just to be safe. I dropped the backpack off at home and went out to buy a scale along with other random items so I wouldn't appear suspicious, because condoms, zip lock bags, beef jerky, a scale, and a pack of gum is not suspicious at all.

I got home and broke the brick apart and started measuring it and weighing out grams. Good thing I just bought a lot of zip lock bags. It turns out the brick Chuck gave me was close to 12 ounces, so I over paid by $140 but why split hairs. It just meant that I would have to sell an ounce for $370 to make an $800 profit. With the brick of weed broken up into smaller bags, all I needed now were clients.

Chapter 6 – The System

Friday morning came and I was ready for happy hour. I invited the same group of friends to happy hour that I usually went out with after work, but then I thought, I can't sell to people I work with, obviously that would jeopardize my job. I would have to get out of my comfort zone and become an extrovert in order to meet complete strangers and ask them if they smoked weed and wanted to buy some, yeah because that's easy to do.

I kept happy hour on the agenda for later but I moved it out to the beach bars instead of the bars close to work. I was hoping to meet some surfers, right, surfers like to smoke weed. Five o'clock came and I had a good day at work, I was able to add 3 new clients to my investment book that day. Not too bad as I now had 9 clients each with a net worth greater than $500,000. My book was close to $5 Million AUM (Assets under Management). I told my friends we were going out to celebrate my 3 new clients. We went to Atlantic Beach and found a bar located right on the beach that looked out to the ocean. We sat down, ordered drinks, and I started scoping out the bar but there wasn't a lot of people there yet. I asked the waitress when they get busy and she told me people start rolling in around 9:00 pm. I told my friends we should grab a bite to eat and then come back here later.

We strolled around the area and went to a great seafood restaurant. I had to use the restroom and it was occupied but when the door opened I smelled weed. I asked the guy coming out "hey do you smoke" and he gave me a strange look and walked by me, yeah probably not the best timing. I went into the bathroom and I could still smell it, the aroma was strong. I looked up and noticed the window was cracked open and thought it has to be coming from outside. I finished my business, washed my hands, and walked out of the bathroom and I exited the restaurant. I headed to the back of the building where two cooks were hanging out having a smoke break. They looked at me and I said "hey, you guys smoke weed?", they turned back to face one another and I stepped a little closer, I leaned in and said "I sell if you guys are ever interested" and the short guy turned his head to me and said "we're good man".

OK, so I didn't make a sell but thinking back to my multi-level marketing days, they use to say you miss one hundred percent of the shots you don't take. I went back into the restaurant and sat down with my friends and ordered my food, shrimp and oysters. After dinner we went to a few other bars in the area, one so smoky I was sure there had to be some future clients there. I played a game of ping pong with a short Pilipino guy named Randy, he was good, but I had some old rusty skills from back in the day when I played my best friend Tyler in his basement. I made a bet with Randy that if he beat me at ping pong I would buy his beer. After I bought Randy his 5th beer I could tell Randy and I were going to be good friends and we played a few game of pool. I looked at my watch and it was already 10:32 pm. Randy asked if we were about to leave and I told him we were about to head to another bar if he'd like to join us. He came with us to the bar at the beach and the place was packed. No longer could you see the ocean because it was so dark and there were so many people there you couldn't hear the sound of the ocean either. Randy knew everyone at the bar and he introduced me and my friends to his friends and acquaintances. We stayed out until 1:30 am and I got Randy's number as well as several ladies numbers thanks to Randy being my wingman.

Randy happened to be a surfer but he also owned a fishing charter company. He had a sweet charter boat located in Mayport and his townhouse was close to the docks as well. I slept in on Saturday and woke up at noon, I hadn't partied that hard in a long time. I called Randy and thanked him for showing us around and introducing me to all of his friends, not to mention being an epic wingman. He said he was having a gathering at his house that night and invited me over. I took an ounce with me in case I met anyone who wanted to buy weed.

I arrived at his townhouse and introduced myself to a few people hanging out by the garage. I walked into the house and saw Randy on the couch with a couple of women next to him and they were taking hits of a joint and passing it around, jackpot! Randy looked over at me and got up, came over and shook my hand and pulled me in for a hug. I thanked him for the invite and said "man, I'm happy you smoke weed because I sell weed". He said "for real, how much do you charge for quarter bag?" and I did the math real quick in my head, $370 divided by 4 is $92.50, so I rounded up. I told Randy I charge $100 which I know is a bit pricey but its top shelf bud, tying to sound like I knew what I was talking about. Again I did my studying by watching movies and reading books. Randy said deal and asked if I had it on me which I replied "I have it in the car, be right back". Again doing the math in my head, 1 ounce equals 28 grams, divided by 4 equals 7. I grabbed 7 dime bags and went back inside.

I don't know why but at that moment I thought back to school when someone asked "when will I ever use math and all this useless knowledge in the real world?" well I was certainly glad I enjoyed math in school. Randy gave me $100, opened the bag and smelled the weed. He smiled at me and said "from now on, I'll buy from you because my current guy is a prick and he's hard to get ahold of, never answers his damn phone". I thanked him and said "feel free to have your friends give me a call anytime". Randy took it out of the bag and placed it on something called Raw rolling papers. He said they were the best papers for rolling a tight joint, aside from Shine 24k rolling papers. He lit up the joint and asked me if I wanted a hit. I told him I actually have never smoked before but appreciated the offer. He said that's cool bro, at least you'll never get high on your own supply. I laughed and said "are you quoting Biggie" and we both started rapping the 10 crack commandments. Randy stopped rapping and said "You're a dope dealer. I'm going to recommend you to all my friends". I said "I'm not dealing dope yet, just weed, but if your friends want it, I can get it".

I did it, Randy was my first client and I made $100, now I just had $4,350 to go. Randy kept his word because the very next day two of his friends called me and asked if they could get the same thing Randy got the night before saying it was the best weed they've ever had. I said I would be right out and I drove back to Atlantic Beach to meet them both at the same time, two birds one stoned, yes I have bad jokes. Each paid me $100 for a Q just as Randy did and one of them asked me if she could buy more tomorrow. I asked how much she wanted to buy and she said an ounce if I had that much. I told her to meet me at the corner of Gate Parkway and Southside and bring $400. She agreed and came through, no muss no fuss. I was excited because I was getting closer and closer to my goal, $700 down and $3,750 to go.

Randy's friends and friend of friends started placing several orders and between managing my client's investments at CES during the day and making rounds after work, I was able to quickly make my goal of selling all 13 ounces at $400 each and I ended up making a profit of $1,700, well above my target. I guess people liked having a reliable and trustworthy dealer or so they said.

I called Chuck and placed another order before I sold everything I had from the first 13 ounces, but this time I picked up double the amount. I was able to move that much weed in a month as Randy took me to several parties in Ponte Vedra, some of his wealthy clients who charted his boat once a month. If I said they smoked a lot of weed, well that would be a huge understatement, they also asked if I would sell other drugs and I told them I would get back to them. I was a bit worried that my wealthy CES clients might be friends with these people or family of my other clientele, so I had to be very careful about what I sold and who I sold it to. I decided to create a system to protect myself and avoid both businesses crossing over.

Now that I had a lot of regular clients I needed to create "code words" for the drugs they wanted to buy just in case I popped up on someone's radar and they started listening to my calls, I wanted to sound like I was doing business, investment recommendations. I hoped that would throw the Feds off or anyone else that was listening. Was I paranoid, yeah probably but now that I started dealing in both weed and cocaine, I needed to make it sound like I was doing legitimate business and that there was no way this clean stand-up guy could be selling drugs.

I gave my regular buyers a business card that read "Invest in the Market. Invest in YOU! Come join our investment club today. We buy in companies like Scotts Weed Killer and Coca-Cola. Call today to schedule an appointment. 904-555-0082". I told them "when you call, don't say your name, just say you're interested in the investment club and would like to possibly buy shares in Scotts or Coca-Cola or both based on which product you want to buy, weed or coke". If they said Scotts Weed Killer. Then I would ask how many shares they were interested in, and they would tell me 1 share for a gram, 14 shares for half an ounce, and 28 shares for an ounce. If they said Coca-Cola, they would go beyond one ounce and ask for 62 shares which got them 2.18 ounces, or 125 shares for 4.40 ounces, 250 shares for a quarter kilo and all the way to 1,000 shares for 35.27 ounces, a kilo.

I gave my regulars extra cards to share with friends and asked if they could pass along the system when placing orders. I told them this system protects me but also protects them as well. Business was booming as I was able to add more clients at CES to my book but they said I had to pass the CFP exam before I could add any more clients. I studied for the exam and paid my $695 to take the CFP as I already had the 4,000 apprentice hours under my belt. I passed the exam with flying colors and a week later I became a certified Discretionary Investment Advisor for CES. I followed the investment model of a longtime Portfolio Manager at CES and I put all 14 clients in a managed product that allowed me to have full discretion (trade authority) on their accounts. Basically this allowed me to set it and forget it and collect an "advisory" fee of 1.25%. I was paid $137,500 a year for having $11,000,000 AUM (Assets under Management). This portfolio management style was perfect as it provided me with the flexibility to run my side business. I was on the phone with clients all day long or sitting in my office watching the markets, just set it, and forget it.

Soon I was pulling in close to $5,825 per month from CES and close to $35,000 per month from selling weed and coke. I called Lisa every week to ask how Sara was doing and to see if she got the money I sent, a thousand a month which was $600 more than what was required by law that I send for child support. I asked Lisa if it would be ok if I came to visit and she kept making excuses why it wasn't a good time. I told her to let me know when it would be a good time because I wanted to come and meet my daughter for the first time. At this point Sara was already seven months old and I felt like I was missing out on her life. Of course I thought about fighting for custody but there was no way I could take care of Sara and do what I do, so I kept at it and put all my money aside to eventually buy a house and a more reliable car.

Chapter 7 – Expansion

Business was good and my clients were using the system. I felt it was time to expand my operations and bring on a partner. Randy had mentioned to me that he wanted to start selling, he said his charter business missed several days because of bad weather and major boat repairs. Randy said "bottom line, I need to buy a new boat". I told Randy I would bring him in but I get 25% of everything he sold for the first year and every year after it goes down 5%. He agreed and wanted to go celebrate so we decided to go to his favorite strip club off of Atlantic Boulevard, the Gold Club. Because I'm cheap I only spent $20, the cover charge to get in. Personally I think strip clubs are a waste of money, why spend good money to give myself blue balls, but Randy loved them. Right when we got into the club Randy popped a pill, he said it was ecstasy and asked if we could start selling ecstasy because all of his friends love it. He said he went to a Festival in Orlando called EDC (Electric Daisy Carnival) and it was everywhere. He said if we got someone down to those Festivals in Tampa and Miami, we could made a killing. I said sure why not and I'd talk to Chuck. He was feeling pretty good at this point and he said he was interested in a girl that worked there, her name was Candy, yes Candy and Randy. He found her and paid for three lap dances, then we headed out after that. On the way home I kept playing a song by T-Pain in honor of Randy and Candy, a song called "I'm in love with a stripper".

The next day I called Chuck and went to his yacht, I told him I needed Weed, Coke, and Ecstasy. Randy started dealing on the side and took over some of my clients which happened to be his friends and I kept all others. He started to build his clientele and created his own system. His clients would call him and solicit interest in fishing. If they want to catch Red Fish they wanted Ecstasy and the number of fish they wanted to catch were the number of pills they wanted. Trout was Weed, 1 was a dime bag, 7 fish was a quarter, and a trophy fish was an ounce. His business started taking off and I was making a pretty penny off of his sales.

At CES I received a few referrals and added two new clients who were High Net Worth.

They both owned their own businesses, one a tech company and the other was a marketing business, and each client had over $2MM (Million) in the market. They were looking for a new Advisor, and I was showing good returns as I put all my clients in a Small Cap Value Fund Portfolio which has netted clients a 31% return over the past 3 years. Word got out and they passed along my name to their friends who happened to be CEO's of other multi-million dollar companies. By the end of November, 2004, I had 28 clients with $29,750,500 Assets under Management (AUM).

I was pulling in $371,000 annually and I sent Lisa $2,500 a month. I called her and told her I would be coming out to see Sara for Christmas. This would be her second Christmas as she was born in on December 29, 2002. I said I planned to be out for Christmas and I wanted to take Sara to meet my parents and celebrate her second birthday since I missed her first birthday. I offered to host a party and I would pay for all of it and surprisingly Lisa agreed to everything. I was so excited and my heart was full of joy. I couldn't wait to hop on a plane to meet my

beautiful baby girl for the first time in person.
I called Randy and asked if he could assist me
with my clients while I was out of town, he
said "I got you covered bro".

On December 23rd I drove my brand new
Jeep Grand Cherokee to the Jacksonville
Airport and I boarded a flight for Denver. I
landed at DIA (Denver International Airport)
at 11:30 AM (MST). I exited the plane and
took the tram to baggage claim, I heard
someone yell my name and when I turned
around there was my brother Spencer who
came to pick me up. We embraced each other
in a hug and waited for my luggage to come
out on the conveyor belt. I grabbed my bags
and we walked to the parking lot, chatting
along the way and catching up with one
another. Not once did I mention I was selling
drugs as a side hustle, no way, my brother
would kill me.

Spencer was working for a large Tech
company in the DTC (Denver Tech Center)
area and became their Chief Marketing
Officer (CMO). He ran their e-mail
marketing campaigns and was working on
integrating with large social media platforms

to reach a broader audience. He had a beautiful home in the Park Meadows area and was in between girlfriends at the moment. He let me stay at his house for the next few days while I visited Lisa and Sara on Christmas Day. I had planned to bring lots of gifts so it was a good thing Spencer lived down the road from the Park Meadows Mall.

I called Lisa to get Sara's clothing size but she told me to buy her toys and give her cash for clothes and she would go buy them. I bought Sara every toy under the sun, I also opened a Roth IRA for Sara right after I found out she was my daughter and started maxing out the contributions as well as managing the investments. I wanted to make sure she was taken care of just in case she needs the money when she's older, plus what's great about a Roth is Sara wouldn't have to pay taxes on it as it's taxed at the time of the contribution, not like a traditional IRA where it's taxed when you take a distribution, which could mean you would pay more in taxes because the owner of the IRA would be in a higher tax bracket. I printed a Certificate that read "Sara's Roth IRA – For a rainy day, or an emergency, or to bail your Dad out of jail".

I woke up Christmas morning and took my brothers car to Lisa's parent's house in Broomfield. The car was packed full of presents and I took $2,500 in cash. As I pulled up to the house there was a brand new Ford F-150 truck in the driveway. I took out several presents and walked up to the door and it opened up with this beautiful little girl hiding behind Lisa's legs, peeking around them to get a glimpse of my smiling face. It was Sara and Lisa stood there with a smile and opened her arms to embrace me in a hug which surprised me as I wasn't sure how she was going to feel about me being there.

I gave Lisa a hug and Sara had a pacifier in her mouth and I could barely see a smile behind it as I reached down to pick her up and give her a hug. The smile turned into a look of I don't know who you are and why are you holding me, but Lisa told Sara it's ok. She said "Sara that's your daddy", and Sara looked at her Mom and looked back at me, then she wiggled like she wanted down. After I put her down she went into the living room where the tree was and I heard several voices coming from the living room. I asked Lisa to take the presents I had and please set them down in the living room for me as I had to get more out of the car.

After I brought in the rest of the presents, I walked them into the living room where I met Lisa's parents and her boyfriend Steve. Her parents were welcoming but her boyfriend wasn't as nice or welcoming. He shook my hand but never smiled and he looked pissed off about something. Maybe he was mad I was there and that Lisa agreed to it. I asked Lisa if Sara could open a few gifts and she said it was fine and asked if I wanted a drink. I said a water please and she headed off to the kitchen and Steve followed her to the kitchen. I sat on the floor staring at my beautiful girl as I waved her over to open a present. She crawled into my lap and sat down right in between my legs, both of us facing the tree and the present, we opened her first present together. It was a stuffed unicorn and the tag read Fluffy, Sara gave it a big hug and stood up with it and took it into the kitchen to show her Mom. I turned to Lisa's parents and smiled and said "I think she likes it". They smiled back and her Mom said we're so glad you're here, and whispered, don't worry about Steve, he'll warm up to you.

Steve and Lisa walked back into the living room and sat down on the couch. I passed out a few gifts to Lisa's parents and I had gotten a gift for Lisa but decided to hold off on giving it to her as I was worried Steve would get jealous. It was a small gift so I put it in my coat pocket next to the cash. As Sara opened a few more gifts I decided to make small talk and asked what Steve did for work and he said he was a General Contractor working in construction. I said "very cool, is that your new Ford out there?" and Steve replied, "No that's Lisa's" and I noticed her face turned red. I thought to myself, if she's still living at home then how can she afford that truck, but then I had no idea what Lisa did for work either. I changed the subject and asked how they met and Lisa said they met at a country bar down the road called the Grizzly Rose, she said "he asked me to dance". Lisa said he was really good at doing the tush push, cha cha slide, and boot scoot'n boogie which I assumed was line dancing. Steve asked if I knew how to dance to country music and I told him I've never been to a country bar in my life. I asked how long they had been dating and Lisa was about to respond but Steve jumped in and said "I've been with Lisa and Sara shortly after Lisa gave birth". I could tell he felt threatened about me being in Sara's life but I wasn't going anywhere and wanted to be a bigger presence in her life.

We took a break and I asked Lisa if we could go outside and talk privately. We went outside and I said "Sara is so beautiful and you've done an amazing job raising her with the help of Steve and your parents". She said thank you and I asked where she was working. She told me she was in between jobs at the moment. I knew she was using the money to pay for her truck and to be honest, I didn't care because she was doing amazing job of raising Sara. I told Lisa I'm so grateful for everything she has done and I reached into my coat pocket and handed her the gift and the envelope with the cash in it. I told her the cash was for clothes, food, and whatever she and Sara needed, and the gift was just a way to say thank you for everything she's done. She opened the gift which was a Tiffany Necklace with two diamond studded hearts, one silver and one gold. The card read "thank you from the bottom of my heart". Lisa teared up and gave me a big hug and whispered in my ear, thank you so much.

We went back inside and I sat there with Sara and opened her remaining presents and played with a few of the toys together. It was by far one of the best days of my life. I hated having to leave but I told Lisa that I would be back on the 27th to take Sara to Longmont to meet my parents and family as my other brother Mark was back from Iraq and he landed a job selling fire protection equipment to fire departments. I gave Sara a big hug and said my goodbyes, Steve even shook my hand and seemed to lighten up a bit after Lisa had a talk with him.

As I drove back to Spencer's house I actually began to cry because I thought about the day I just had with Sara and I already started to miss her, even though I would see her on the 27th. I have never felt so much love in my life. It was almost hard to drive with my eyes full of tears. I got back to Spencer's house and quickly called Randy to check in and wish him a Merry Christmas. Randy said everything was going well and he had some good news for me. I said spill it and he told me he has three of his friends who want to start dealing for me. I asked him if he knows these people really well, enough to trust them and he said with his life, so I said I'm comfortable with it if he is and we'd talk about when I got back. I told Randy I was lucky to have him as a friend and I thanked him for helping me out in my time of need.

I spent the 26th seeing friends and former co-workers. I even spent time with Ryan, his wife, and their son, but I couldn't stop thinking about Sara and I counted down the minutes until I could see her again on the 27th. Finally the 27th came and Spencer and I went to Lisa's house to pick up Sara. Lisa was there and she helped me get the car seat into my brother's car. Sara came out of the house holding the Unicorn I got her for Christmas and she was hugging it as she walked towards us. I smiled and bent down to pick her up. I kissed her on the cheek and my heart was filled with joy to hold her in my arms. Spencer came over and shook her hand and said "hello baby girl" and she took a quick liking to him as she reached out for him to hold her. I put her in the car seat, gave Lisa a hug goodbye, and we hit the road for Longmont.

We arrived in Longmont and I was a bit nervous the entire way, I'm pretty sure I told my brother he was driving way to fast when he was really only going 5 MPH over the speed limit. I even made him pull over so I could check Sara's pull up diaper and I also wanted to sit in the back seat with her to entertain her. We got out of the car at my parent's house and we walked in to a house full of family members. My Mom and Dad started crying and my brother Mark was dating a girl named Jennifer and she had a little girl of her own named Lacy who was close to Sara's age, just a bit older. My parents welcomed us in and we went to the living room and Sara explored the house with Lacy. They found a few toys to play with and we all sat in the living room watching the kids play with toys and caught up with one another.

They asked how everything went on Christmas and I told them about Lisa, her parents, and her boyfriend Steve. Mom asked how work was going, I told her everything was going great at CES and how quickly I was able to acquire clients. I said my plan was to become the number one Financial Advisor in the southeast region by next summer. I mentioned I was making good money and hoped to buy a house soon. My parents asked about Lisa giving me joint custody and if I had plans to fight for joint custody. I told them I was thinking about it but with my busy schedule it's hard to find time and my Mom stopped me right there, she said you don't find time you make time and you make it work, just look at us, we did fine. I told her it's easier with two parents than just one and who knows if I will ever get married. We had a late lunch and I told my family we had to leave soon to get back to Denver before dark. I was glad my brothers girlfriend Jennifer was there as she helped me with Sara. I had her diaper bag with me but I had never changed a diaper or a pull up in my life. Jennifer saved me as I was about to wipe back to front and she taught me to wipe her from front to back. I would have been in big trouble if I brought her back with a rash or worse.

I called Lisa to tell her we were on our way and leaving Longmont. I gave everyone a hug and carried Sara out to the car and we hit the road for Denver. We got back to Lisa's at 6:30 and I told her everything we did and how Sara got to play with Lacy. I told her how Jennifer, my brother's girlfriend, saved me from disaster as I almost wiped her back to front instead of front to back. Lisa laughed and said rookie mistake. She thanked me for taking care of her and admitted it was a nice break but she missed her every minute she was gone. I asked Lisa about the party on the 29th and she said she forgot and she and Steve planned a trip to Estes Park with Sara for her birthday. I got a bit upset and said "I told you on the phone I wanted to throw her a birthday party". Lisa apologized and said she forgot and asked if I could stay for New Years and throw a party then. I told her my flight leaves on the 30th and I needed to get back to Florida for work. I made a snide remark "you know, the job that pays for that truck right there". She knew I was mad and rather than admitting her mistake, she seemed more concerned about upsetting Steve. I asked if I could come back tomorrow to spend time with Sara before I have to leave and she said they're leaving in the morning and will be gone for 2 days. That pissed me off even more, I said "you know I'm in town until the 30th and wanted to have a party for Sara, you even agreed to it, but you obviously don't care so it looks like I'll have to take you to court and fight to get joint custody". Lisa looked shocked and said "do whatever you want" and took Sara inside and slammed the door shut.

Again, I felt like she ripped my heart out and held it in her hand as I stood there watching her hold it while it was beating. My brother said "What a bitch. That was heartless". We got in the car and as we drove off I noticed Sara climbed up on the couch in the living room to look out the window. I smiled and waved, but my heart sank in my chest and tears started welling up in my eyes. My brother drove us to his house and we opened up a bottle of beer he had saved for my trip back to Colorado called Utopias, I guess he thought I needed a good stiff drink. We hung out for the next two days, mostly hitting the slopes again and going to breweries and getting shit faced, which took my mind off of missing Sara. The 30th arrived and Spencer drove me to the airport and dropped me off.

I gave him a big hug and I got on the plane to go back to Jacksonville.

When I landed and got in my Jeep, Randy called me and said "Welcome back to Jax, now let's go party, I have some news for you". We went to an old Irish Pub in Jacksonville Beach and he told me about his three friends who wanted to deal and said one lives in Savannah, one in Ponte Vedra, and one in Orlando. He said he also has a friend who lives in Miami who might want in, but thought that might be too far and I said "FedEx is the #1 distributor in the US", let's add him to the list. In my mind I thought as long as I could keep the money coming in, I would need a bigger place to store all this cash. The very next day I decided to take out a home loan as I had money in the bank for a down payment and my credit was good. I figured with my CES income I could easily get approved for a house in Julington Creek, a suburb of Jacksonville full of middle class families. I mean if I'm going to play the part of an up and coming Financial Advisor then I needed to look the part. The area was known for having great daycares and schools just in case I was able to get full custody of Sara in the near future.

I was approved for a loan and bought a house. I asked a few co-workers along with Randy and a few of his friends to help me move as I had acquired a bit of furniture over these past few years. My closest work friend named Fred came over to help along with Randy and two of his friends. We got everything moved in five hours and I returned the rental truck and took the boys out for beers and pizza. Fred was also a Financial Advisor at CES but wasn't doing so well. He wasn't able to build his book as fast as I built mine. He told me his daughter was diagnosed with POTS (Postural Orthostatic Tachycardia Syndrome) and the medical expenses were piling up as he had to take her to the Mayo Clinic in Rochester Minnesota to see a bunch of specialists and get a treatment plan for her. He was worried about losing his house and possibly his wife as they argue about money constantly and he thought she was going to take the kids and leave. I had a few beers in me and I felt bad for him so I asked if he wanted to make some money on the side. I hesitated to tell him as I work with him, but I knew I could trust him so I said "listen I can connect you with a guy if you'd be interested in selling weed on the side". Fred looked at me and said "hell yeah, I know a lot of people that smoke and I'll do whatever it takes to save my family, who do you know?". I told him I had a connection and could get him whatever he needs. I usually gave all of my new dealers the same deal I gave Randy when he started, but I let Fred keep all of his profits because I felt bad for him and his situation. Fred said he was all in and now I had a total of 6 dealers beneath me. Funny how multi-level marketing works in the real world and the drug world. Always someone above you and to be successful you need people below you doing the exact same thing you did.

I was just about to call Chuck and tell him I was going to come by when I received a call from Todd telling me Chuck had passed away, heart attack, and now Chuck and Todd's connection, Carlos, wanted me to be his distributor for the area. He gave me the number to Carlos and said I needed to call him right away. I noticed it was a Miami area code and I placed the call. Carlos answered and said "so you're Chuck's guy the Stock

Broker?" I had no idea how he knew that as I never told Chuck what I did for work but I said "Yeah, I'm the Financial Advisor and you're…" and he cut me off, "come to Miami tomorrow and meet me at 4:00 PM, I'll text you the address", then he hung up the phone. The next day I packed a few things and drove down to Miami. Straight down 95 and it took me five hours to get there. I left Jacksonville at 8:00 am as I had never been to Miami and I wanted to spend a little time looking around. The great thing about being a Financial Advisor is you make your own schedule and work wherever you want to work, so it wasn't suspicious for me to say I'm meeting a client in Miami for a round of golf.

I only had a few hours to kill so I decided to checkout Ocean Drive, Miami Beach and South Beach. It just so happens the address Carlos gave me was for a hotel in South Beach called 1 Hotel South Beach. It was 3:30 PM EST and I arrived early and went to the bar to get a drink to ease my nerves. I couldn't believe I was here. I ordered a mojito and took it with me outside where the view was stunning, both the ocean and the women around the pool, they looked like super models, not to mention this mojito was the best damn mojito I've ever had. For a minute I felt like I was way over my head being here and started to panic on the inside but just then my cell phone rang and I answered it. Carlos said "I see a goofy looking white guy in front of me wearing a polo shirt, jeans, and flip flops, please tell me that's not you". I turned around to see this well-dressed man wearing a sharp looking Armani Suit, tailored perfectly to fit him, with a cell phone in his hand as he handed it to a very large muscular man dressed in all black next to him. He walked up and shook my hand and said "I'm going to call you CJ for Charles Junior. Welcome to the family CJ" and he pulled me in close for a hug.

Carlos asked me to follow him to the elevators with the very large man right by his side. We got on the elevator and headed up to his room. We exited the elevator and walked down the hallway, a door opened and another large muscular man dressed in black held the door open and Carlos walked in and I followed. I heard the door close behind me and the two large men stood by the door. Carlos looked at me and said strip. I knew he wanted me to take off my shirt to make sure I wasn't wearing a wire but he actually wanted me to take all of my clothes off. I didn't hesitate and took everything off, my polo shirt, jeans and underwear, he did say strip. As I stood there naked in front of a man I just met and with two large men behind me, I felt very vulnerable. He smiled and said "you take orders well and you're in good shape, do you work out?", as I started putting my clothes back on I told him I hit the gym here and there, but I don't have a lot of time between work and my other activities. He asked me to come out on the balcony with him and enjoy the view so I followed Carlos through the doors, he reached for two glasses and he offered me a drink of champagne, a toast to new relationships. Carlos said he liked me a lot and asked how many people I had working for me, I replied six and have people spread out over Florida and one in Savannah. We stood there looking out over the beach with yachts cruising by on the ocean, they were everywhere. He looked at me and smiled then said "I like you CJ, we're about to make a lot of money".

Chapter 8 – Lavish Living

Carlos was right, I started pulling in close to $90,000 a month, and to ensure my anonymity I created a similar system as before, I had my dealers call me pretending to be actual clients I had in my book of business at CES. They would inquire about buying stocks which I had created code names for, such as Facebook was Weed, Apple was Ecstasy, Coke was Coke, and we never sold meth or any other drugs, we kept it simple. Every month as I reviewed my client's investments, I would send a note to my dealers whenever I changed the code names which I did on a regular basis as I constantly made changes to my CES portfolio. I also acquired more clients at CES and became the number one advisor in the region. I was asked to be interviewed by Money Magazine about my portfolio management style. That was cool and my parents called me right away saying they bought everyone they knew a copy of the magazine. My Mom said she was so proud of me and my accomplishments.

I was making $350,000 per year selling drugs but I needed to find a way to clean the money coming in from my dealers. I decided to fly back to Colorado as they just legalized Marijuana for recreational use and I bought a dispensary, actually two of them. My plan was to launder the drug money through a legal Marijuana business through a process called Placement. Placement is when criminal proceeds such as drug money is introduced to the financial system without attracting the attention of the financial institutions or local law enforcement. I hired two women to run the dispensaries and I sat them both down and explained my purpose of buying both businesses. I needed to be upfront and honest and I told them they would be compensated very well. Both said they had no issues with it and I let them know I would be shipping the drug money to them, they would take the clean money and send it back to me and use the drug money for the dispensary business and blend it into the cash we kept in the safes as dispensaries aren't able to make deposits at the bank. That way my income appears to be clean from the stores I own. As we cut checks or invoices between businesses we further "layer" the funds which creates more confusion as to origin of the funds in order to make us appear legitimate, that process is called layering. You might be asking, where did you learn about this process? At CES of course, they make us take mandatory classes for anti-money laundering and explain the process to make us aware in case we see this type of activity occurring, we have to report it.

I hired the rest of my crew to assist with running the dispensaries and while I was in Colorado I tried to call Lisa to see if I could see Sara as she had told me via text message that I'll never get to see her again, and she declined my call again and sent me a text saying "stop calling". That was the straw that broke the camel's back and I tried to obtain custody but Colorado favored Lisa and awarded her full custody as she and Steve were now married. I still continued to send money even though I knew not all of it went directly to Sara. I started putting money aside in one of my personal investment accounts and I also continued to contribute to her Roth IRA.

By the end of the year I had made over $1 Million selling drugs and was on track to triple that amount as I added two more dealers who were hungry and started moving heavy weight. Both lived in Tampa and one said he had a lot of clients in Key West. I drove down to Tampa to visit them and it happened to be the same weekend as the Gasparilla Pirate Festival. Will and John, my new dealers took me to the "Parade of Pirates" which reminded me of Mardi Gras as they threw beads, treasures, and doubloons. There was lot of rum being passed around and several scantily clad women, but it wasn't my scene as I couldn't stand drunken idiots trying to pick a fight with me for no reason. It was a lot of fun but I wanted to see the city of Tampa and St Pete. Will and John stayed back to push product at the festival and I decided to get a hotel room on the beach in Clearwater. I chartered a boat and went fishing for Yellowfin Tuna and Mahi-Mahi as both were running at that time in the Gulf of Mexico. It was a chance for me to clear my head and relax a bit, but there wasn't much relaxation as we kept getting hits on the line and caught fish after fish after fish. We caught Mahi, Yellowfin, and I also caught a Spanish Mac and a Cobia. When we got back the guides fileted the fish for me and I took the meat back with me to the hotel in my cooler.

I got back to my room and put the fish in the refrigerator and took a hot shower. I got cleaned up and headed down to the lobby bar where I met the most beautiful woman I have ever met in my life named Dayana. I was getting a drink before heading out to the beach. I introduced myself and she asked if I'd like to join her for a drink. I told her I was going to take a walk on the beach before the sun went down and asked her if she'd like to join me. She accepted and we both grabbed our drinks and headed to the beach. Dayana had long dark hair, brown eyes, and looked just like Penelope Cruz, I jokingly asked if she was Penelope, saying she looked just like her and Dayana said she got that all the time. I told her I thought Penelope was gorgeous and I'm sure it's meant to be a compliment of her beauty, she smiled and thanked me. As we walked on the beach heading North with the Gulf of Mexico to our left, I asked the usual questions like where are you from and what do you do for work. She said "I'm from Nicaragua, but I currently live Redwood City, California. I'm the CTO for a startup called

1K, it's a photo and video sharing app were our users create photo albums for events like weddings, birthday parties, sports events, etc., and then you share the code with family, friends, sports fans, to invite them to add their photos to the album. We also have a cool map feature so you can see what's happening around the world. She handed me a card that read, 1K App: Because a picture is worth a thousand words. Available on Android and IOS. Learn more about 1K at www.1kapp.io. She said "I'm here to pitch it to the Tampa Bay Buccaneers to use it for their games". I had a look of amazement written all over my face and she asked what I did for a living. I told her I was a drug dealer and then I laughed and I said "I was just trying to top yours". She laughed and I told her I'm a Financial Advisor for CES and I made a yawning motion with my hands. She said I looked familiar and she's actually heard of me as she read an article about my portfolio management style in Money Magazine. She told me she's an avid investor in the market and asked if I could give her any tips. We both laughed and I couldn't stop looking at her beautiful smile.

I was shocked someone actually read that article and more shocked by the fact she was standing in front of me, so kind and sweet. We talked some more but started to head back to the hotel as the sun was setting. We arrived at the hotel just in time to sit on the beach and watch the sky light up in shades of red and orange, it was the most beautiful sunset I have ever seen in my life. I looked over at Dayana and her eyes were straight forward, focused on the sunset, then she turned to me and said "isn't it amazing" and all of the sudden I got butterflies in my stomach. I looked back at the orange glow of the sky and told her I have never seen a sunset like that in my life and not to sound cheesy but I've never met anyone like her in my life either. I asked if she'd like to grab a bite to eat and she nodded yes. We walked back into the hotel and she said she wanted to clean up a bit, to meet her back in the lobby in an hour. I went back to my room and took the fastest shower of my life. I heard the phone in my room ring and it was Dayana asking if it was ok if we kept the dress casual, I agreed and decided to wear shorts, boat shoes, and a nice dress shirt. I headed to the lobby and noticed Dayana was there waiting for me. She smiled and said "what took you so long" and we both laughed, I told her I apologize for being so high maintenance. We headed towards the front and I asked if she likes seafood and Italian food, she said she loves both so we headed to a restaurant called Sea-Guini. We got a table with a view of the Gulf and ate the most delicious food. Dayana and I had great conversation and both confessed to be single and she told me more about her app and how they just launched on Android and IOS. I have an Android phone so I opened the Play Store and downloaded the app, she even showed me how to use it by creating a public album, sharing our location, which put the album on the "Public Album Map" feature in the app. She said anyone using 1K could find the album on the map and add their photos of their experience at Sea-Guini.

Dayana liked to joke around and our humor seemed to match well with one another, we went back to the hotel and had a few drinks at the bar before we called it a night. The attraction was there and I walked her back to her room and gave her a kiss on the cheek and asked if I could see her again tomorrow. She told me she was pitching to the Tampa Bay Buccaneers and then she had to catch a flight back to California. I made a frown and asked if I could call her and come visit sometime. She said she would really like that and gave me her phone number and we told each other goodnight. I headed back to my room and as I laid in bed, all I could think about was her, her smile, her beautiful eyes, and how funny she was. I eventually fell asleep and woke up the next day, thinking about her. I opened the 1K app and clicked on View Album to look at the photos we took last night at the restaurant. I sent her a text that said "Good luck with the pitch today, I hope you get a touchdown. Safe travels and talk to you soon". She texted back right away with "Thank you, I really enjoyed last night and I hope we can get together again soon".

I was about to drive back to Jacksonville when I drove by a car dealership. I saw this black Porsche 911 Turbo Wide Body and I had to stop and take a look. I took it for a test drive and bought it on the spot and traded in the Jeep. As I headed back to Jacksonville in my new ride, I couldn't stop thinking about Dayana and then my mind shifted to Sara. I tried to call Lisa again and this time she answered, I asked about Sara and she said everything was fine with Sara, however she and Steve were getting a divorce. She said he was having an affair with a young college girl who works at the country bar they met at. I told her I was sorry to hear about that, and she said I could stop sending money as she was getting half of everything Steve owned which was plenty for her and Sara. I said I would continue to send money as I would like for her to save it up for Sara's first car and college, even though I had plenty of money put aside for both, I just wanted a reason to send money and take care of Sara. Lisa asked if I wanted to come out and visit. I said I'd love to and I also told her I had bought a few dispensaries and will be out in a week. She said Sara's getting big and she'll be excited to see her daddy. We hung up the phone and I found myself doing 98 MPH on I-4 quickly approaching Orlando. I drove by Disney and thought about how great it would be to bring Sara and possibly Dayana on a trip there sometime in the near future.

When I got back to Jacksonville I decided to buy my own boat, a small yacht similar to the one Chuck had. The money was flowing in and if I was going to be CJ (Chuck Junior) then I had to play the part, plus I really enjoyed fishing and being out on the water. Now that I had 8 dealers working for me and they all followed my system, along with my dispensaries to launder the money, I had a bit of time to focus on my investment strategy. I made a few changes to my portfolio and now offered several strategies, long term and short term gain strategies. CES allowed me to sell my strategies to other investors. I disclosed my "outside business activities" and they fully approved my dispensaries as I was making the company a lot of money. I was now number eight on the top ten list of Financial Advisors in the United States. My goal was to make top 5 by year end. I managed my own personal accounts and was making money from my clients at CES, my dealers, my investments, and my dispensaries. I was on my way to make $3.5 Million that year. I started washing money through Randy's fishing charter and his new clothing line business, Randy's Reds Fishing Gear. Fred's wife's bakery located near downtown in Riverside, and I bought some properties and rented space for local businesses located in Springfield, which was just north of downtown Jacksonville, and considered to be an up and coming area.

I called Dayana and asked when I could come visit her and she said she wanted to come to Jacksonville and see where I lived, if that was ok. I said we can try to set up a meeting with the Jaguars while you're here and she said the entire NFL picked up the 1K app and planned to start using it for all of their games and events. I told her we have to celebrate that huge win and it just so happens I'm in the market for a new house, I asked if she would come out and assist me. She said she'd love to and just bought her ticket to come out on Saturday. She sent me her flight information and I said I couldn't wait to see her, then we said our goodbyes.

I wanted to appear sophisticated for Dayana and not a wealthy asshole that drove a Porsche because you know what they say, what's the difference between a Porsche and a Porcupine? On a Porcupine the pricks are on the outside. So I decided to head over to the Mercedes dealership and I bought a new C-Class with all the bells and whistles. I had the Porsche, the Yacht, and new C-Class and was about to buy a new house in Ponte Vedra on the beach. I couldn't believe how far I had come already and it appeared it wasn't going to stop any time soon, and I'm ok with that. Carlos was happy with me and my dealers were killing it out there, I was on a natural high and crazy excited to see Dayana this weekend.

It was Friday and I picked out three houses for us to look at on Saturday. Just as I pulled into my driveway I receive a call from Lisa asking if I was able to fly out this weekend to see Sara. I told her I had already made plans as I have a friend flying in from out of town and Lisa got upset and said "obviously your daughter comes second to your plans" and she hung up the phone. I tried to call her right back but she declined my call. I was upset and just then Dayana called to ask if she could stay until Tuesday as she had a conference in Orlando to attend. I told her that just made my day as I was not having a very good day at all. I asked her if she had ever been to Savannah and she replied no, which I replied "fantastic, then we'll spend a day in Savannah as I have never been there either". It just so happened that my dealer in Savannah said he was having car issues and needed an extra supply until he could get it fixed.

Saturday came and so did the butterfly's I had felt before. I drove my new C-Class to the airport and parked it in the garage. I went to baggage claim and waited, in a few minutes I saw her coming down the escalator wearing this amazing red and white floral dress. She saw me, smiled and waved, and walked over and gave me a big hug. We waited to get her suitcase and made small talk, how was your flight, any issues with the layover in Atlanta, and then her suitcase popped out. We grabbed the suitcase, and walked to the car, and put it in the trunk. Dayana said "wow that's a big trunk, I bet you fit a lot of drugs in here". I gave her strange look and she said "remember, you said you were a drug dealer" and then I smiled and laughed, thinking to myself, holy crap, I thought she somehow knew.

We got in the car and she said she booked a hotel room at the Omni Downtown. I assumed she didn't want to come off presumptuous. And I insisted she cancel and stay with me if she was okay with that. She pulled her phone out of her pocket and sent a text and looked over at me and said, cancelled. I told her I was excited she was here and I was looking forward to her opinion on the three houses I had picked out for the day. We drove to the first one and met the Realtor, it was a 4 bed / 3 Bath for $765,000, it was smaller than all the other houses around it but it was on the beach. Dayana said she liked it and thought it was nice but needed a lot of work. I declined on that house and asked to see the second house. We drove to the address provided by the realtor and it was a gated property and located high on the sand dunes as if it was built up to rise above the rest. It was a gorgeous 5 bedroom / 4 ½ bath with stunning views of the ocean and modern appliances. It had a 4 car garage and a mother-in-law suite built above the garage. The asking price was $1,095,000 and I asked the agent if the third one topped this one and she said it was similar to the first, so I said I'd take this one. Dayana was down by the infinity pool that looked out to the ocean and I was on the second story balcony so I yelled down to her and asked her what she thought. She yelled up to me that she loved it, I turned and shook the realtors hand and nodded, this is the one.

As Dayana and I drove back to my house in Julington Creek she asked if I really planned to buy that house or if I was just showing off. I told her I've always dreamt of living in a house on the beach since I was a teenager reading Rob Report Magazines, and now I could finally afford to make that dream a reality. She grabbed my hand and smiled and said "I'm proud of you" and I smiled back and said "I still can't believe it's going to be mine. I also can't believe you're here with me and I'm so grateful for that". We got to the house and took her luggage inside. I set her luggage on the bed and turned around and Dayana was standing right there, she gently grabbed the back of my neck and pulled me in for a passionate kiss. When we stopped kissing she pushed the suitcase off the bed and laid down while pulling me on top of her and I kissed her again, her fingers busy undoing the buttons on my shirt and unbuckling my belt. We stopped kissing and we stood up so I could help her unzip her beautiful red and white dress which fell to the floor and there she stood in while lacy panties and a white bra. I unclasped her bra and she turned around and laid back down on the bed. I took off my unbuttoned shirt, pants, shoes, and socks. Dayana arched her back and I helped her slide off her panties and I took off my boxers. We had the most passionate sex I have ever had in my life. We made love all night long and took a few breaks, naked trips to the kitchen for food and drinks. We even made love in the kitchen while having dessert, ice cream with chocolate syrup and whip cream, which we licked off one another. Things got a little messy so we jumped in the shower, washing each other off. Dayana and I went back to bed and laid down and watched a little TV and we passed out in each other's arms. I was in heaven with an angel at my side.

Sunday arrived and I came into the bedroom with breakfast. I made a little bit of everything as I didn't know what Dayana liked to eat, turns out she likes eggs, bacon, and waffles, everything I like. We got dressed and packed and overnight bag, then we got in the C-Class and headed off to Savannah. Only a two hour drive, Dayana and I shared our life stories with one another. She was born in Nicaragua and her Dad was an accountant for the government and her Mom was a kindergarten teacher. She has two older brothers, one was a dentist in Nicaragua and another who was looking for work in states. I asked what he wants to do and she said he's into tech like her and applying for Google. She told me he currently lives with her in their two bedroom apartment. I told her about my family and upbringing, I even told her the 4th of July story, but I didn't mention anything about Sara and Lisa, not just yet.

We arrived in Savannah and I told her I had to drop off a package, a box of books for a friend of mine at the Savannah College Art and Design (SCAD). We swung by the school and I met my dealer and gave him the box, he gave me a backpack full of cash and darted off. I put the backpack in the trunk and we headed to the Kehoe House, a historic Bed and Breakfast. We got to the B&B and I told Dayana to head in while I got the luggage.

We checked in and decided to venture out to the historic district for some drinks at Chuck's Bar, which made me think of Chuck, and then we got some food at the Chart House. After walking down River Street for a bit we headed to Forsyth Park where we laid in the grass and watched people come and go, in between our make out sessions. It was starting to get dark so we headed back to the B&B to clean up as we booked reservations for a Ghost Tour that evening. As the tour was a bar hopping tour with some pretty intriguing stories and no signs of ghosts, both Dayana and I were pretty buzzed so we decided to head back to the bed and breakfast and ordered in. After dinner Dayana and I spent the rest of the night making love, I was falling in love with her and it scared me because of the way Lisa rejected me in the past. I promised myself I wouldn't put up my defenses and if I decided to go all in, then I would be 100% all in.

Dayana and I woke up in each other's arms again and took another shower together before heading down for breakfast. We packed up the car and headed back to Jacksonville. I told Dayana I wanted to take her out on my boat and try our hand at fishing. She said she loved fishing so we spent all day Monday on the boat. Dayana commented about my lavish lifestyle and asked how I could afford it all. I told her about my dispensaries and rental properties in Springfield, also my investments. I made no mention of the drugs, not until things got serious between us. Dayana bought it and said she had always dreamt of owning a boat, so I said it's yours if you want it. She smiled and said wrap it up and ship it to Cali. I told her the price of ownership meant she had to stay here with me in Jacksonville. She said "I'll think about it and give you an answer after my conference ends in Orlando". The day flew by and we were both exhausted from being in the sun all day. We caught a nice sized flounder, seven Redfish, and a Black Drum. When we arrived home, I cleaned and fileted the fish for dinner. Dayana made a salad and we were so tired we took dinner to bed and passed out at 9:30 PM. I woke up to Dayana's hand caressing my body and we began to kiss, I rolled over on top of her and kissed her neck, then her chest and stomach, and worked my way down. The sex was great and full of passion, I didn't want to let her go.

She asked if I could drive her down to Orlando that morning for her conference, I looked deep into her beautiful brown eyes and said "I think I'm falling in love with you and I don't want you to go". She replied "I feel the same but I have to go, it's my job". We got in the Porsche and I drove her down to the Dolphin Hotel near Disney.

We walked into the lobby and she checked in. We looked at each other and both leaned in for a kiss and a hug. I said "I love you and I'm going to miss you". Dayana started to cry and I began to tear up. She said "I love you too and I'll see you soon" as she kissed me one last time and headed off toward the elevator doors that were open. As she got in the elevator, the tears began to fall down my cheek.

Chapter 9 – King of the Hill

Dayana flew back to California after her conference and we travelled back and forth for almost a full year. Dayana and I flew to Tampa and we made reservations at Sea-Guini where I proposed and she accepted, and we stayed at the same hotel we met at that night. Another year later Dayana and I got married and had our wedding on the beach. After two years of being married, we got pregnant with identical twins, two boys named James and Timothy (Tim). Sara was now 18 and headed off to college at CSU (Colorado State University) where she wants to become a Spanish Teacher. She spent summers with us in Florida and learned Spanish from Dayana, especially during our trips to Disney World. Lisa and I got along over the past 10 years and Dayana and I made several trips to Colorado to visit her and Sara. We would take trips to the mountains and I invited Lisa and Sara to join us on vacations to Vail, Breckenridge, and Aspen. We also bought a house in Telluride as business was booming and I had dealers located in eight major cities; Chicago, New York, New Jersey, Los Angeles, Denver, Dallas, Detroit, and Philadelphia.

I was ranked #2 on the Forbes Top Advisor Rankings list as my Team Assets (Custodied) hit $4.6 Billion with a minimum account size of $25 Million and typical size of household accounts are $25 to $100 Million. As a team we brought in $56 Million and my take home from CES that year exceeded $30 million. My goal was to become #1 by next year and beat the top Advisor at $7.3B. So why sell drugs to dealers and take the risk, it's a fair question and honestly I had been doing it for so long it wasn't hard work and it paid very well. With my network of dealers I had made close to $50 Million over the past 10 years and all of my audits at CES came back clean and my lifestyle appeared to be supported by my day job so my lavish lifestyle appeared normal in the eyes of the IRS. Along with my investments and Sara's Roth, I had over $80 Million in my accounts. My net worth was over $160 Million, but it wasn't enough, I wanted more, a lot more.

With the dispensaries doing so well I decided to purchase land in Colorado and Massachusetts to begin growing my own cannabis farms. I opened a few dispensaries in Boston as well, that way I was able to sell weed legally in those two states. Dayana set up a headquarters in Jacksonville for her company, the 1K app (because a picture is worth a thousand words) which also became the number one app on the Google Play Store and the Apple Store. She was promoted to CEO of the company making $720,000 annually with bonuses totaling $4.5 Million. Dayana wanted to invest in an AR company out of Canada because they were leading the way on AR Advertising, and it just so happens they promote companies that sell cannabis through the use of Augmented Reality and hologram videos. She offered them their first seed round and worked with other Female Owned and Managed Venture Capital Companies and General Partners to offer a Series A round of funding for $75 Million.

I was living the life of my dreams and was able to buy everything I had ever dreamt of since I was a teenager. I felt like I was living the life I would see in my Rob Report magazines because I bought a Bugatti Chiron (16-Cylinder, 4 Turbo Charger, 1,500 Horse Power) for a mere $3 Million. Dayana wanted the new McLaren 600LT Spider and I bought her one for her birthday. We also bought an island in Belize called Clear Water Caye, 567 acres, for $10 Million. I saw it as an investment as I planned on renting it out throughout the summers but also had plans to build a private house on the island. We had the island cleaned up and ready for the summer. Dayana built the house of her dreams on the opposite side of the island. We also bought a few boats and wave runners for the guests who rented the main cabins and we tried to go as often as possible. We would use a private jet company to fly us there and back. Dayana loved it there because it's a very short flight to Nicaragua to see her family.

I've made Carlos a lot of money and we became close friends, so close he decided to introduce me to the main supplier in Medellin, Columbia named Miguel. We decided to meet at my island and I flew to Miami to meet Carlos, we took a Gulfstream 650 from Miami to Belize City, then took a boat over to Clear Water Caye. We spent the afternoon on the beach having drinks and waited for Miguel to arrive. Carlos told me he's not a typical drug lord, he's not crazy and wild like the others but rather focused on growth and business.

He said I better watch out or he'll turn my island into a farm and factory.

Miguel arrived by boat and he was all by himself, the guy driving the boat left and Miguel was walking towards us down the dock, he was in good shape and looked a lot like the most interesting man in the world, the original Dos Equis guy. Carlos told me not to be nervous, I was nervous because I wanted to make a good impression and yes, I wanted Miguel to like me. He walked up to us, took off his sun glasses, looked into my eyes and shook my hand with a firm handshake. He turned to Carlos and shook his hand and looked at the both of us and said "It's great to finally get the three of us together, now let's go sit down and get the fuck out of this hot sun".

We walked over to the cabana and sat down in the shade. One of my waiters on the island, Roberto, came over and asked us what we wanted to drink. Miguel asked for a beer with a slice of lime and Carlos and I ordered mojitos, because he and I love mojitos. The waiter walked away and Miguel looked at us and said "okay gentlemen let's take a walk and talk business" so we got up and started walking on the white sandy beach and Miguel started back up "so we have 961 packages of cocaine, weighing approximately 1,126.8 kilograms and 38,000 pounds of marijuana that we have to move this month. Unfortunately Carlos, a few of your dealers have gotten caught selling our drugs in Liberty City, Miami and now they're in the custody of the police. How do you plan to handle this, again, since this is not the first time?" Carlos was about to speak when Miguel quickly pulled out 9 millimeter gun and shot him in the head. I jumped to the right and fell into the water with blood on the left side of my body, sitting in the sand I watched as Carlos' body fell to the ground. I was sitting there as the waves kept crashing into me, in shock and my hands were shaking, Miguel could tell I had never experienced anything like this before in my life. I saw Roberto, the waiter, off in the distance about to head our way as I'm sure he heard the gun shot and I waved him off. Miguel looked at me and said "Don't worry, we'll take care of it. Carlos's dealers were about to confess to the Feds who their supplier was and I had to stop that from happening. No one to rat out if there's no rat, besides Carlos was down 47% in sales for the year and I need you to take his place. Carlos told me you have a clean system in place and you've bought land in Colorado and Massachusetts to grow "legal marijuana" and he laughed, "I would like to make you my partner, not just a supplier because you're smart man, a business man, just like me. And Carlos, well he was bad for business. Do we have a deal my friend?" I shook his hand and told him we had a deal. I think I was more afraid of being shot in the head if I said no.

Miguel asked if I had a boat close by and if I'd like to go fishing. I said I had a 35 foot sc-sportcoupe boat on my private dock. He asked me to bring it around to the docks near us and we'll get rid of Carlos and try to catch some fish while we're at it. I couldn't believe he had such little regard for life when Carlos was just telling me how Miguel wasn't crazy and wild like other drug lords, but he definitely was. I took my clothes off except my boxers and walked further into the ocean to wash off the blood on my face, arms, and hands. I told Miguel I would leave my clothes there with him as I didn't want my staff to see anything, even though they probably heard the gun shot from the Main Villa next to the large Palapa. I told him I would also grab him some clothes to change into. I ran to my private cottage and quickly changed into clothes and grabbed a pair of clothes for Miguel. I sprinted to the boat on my private dock and drove it around the public dock and tied it off. Miguel was back at the cabana finishing his beer and I noticed he was on the phone. Right as I walked up he hung up the phone and I handed him the change of clothes. He changed quickly and I grabbed our clothes and put them in a bag I brought with me. I tied the bag around my belt and I grabbed Carlos's wrists and Miguel grabbed his ankles and we carried him out to the boat, the waves washed away all the blood on the beach. I was hoping my staff didn't notice but in the excitement of the moment I forgot to tell them to stay inside. I looked at the large Palapa and noticed Roberto standing there watching us.

We headed out to sea and found a secluded spot, not a single boat around us. Miguel asked if I had a knife on the boat and I went into cabin and grabbed the largest knife I had on the boat and handed it to Miguel. He told me to get my fishing pole ready as he was about to chum the water and he started cutting off pieces and throwing them into the water. I felt nauseous and threw up over the side of the boat and Miguel started to laugh. He said "so gringo, you've never killed anyone before? What about an animal, have you ever shot a dear and cut it open to get the meat?" I told him I have never experienced anything like this before in my life and it's hard because Carlos and I had become friends over the past 10 years, not super close, but he would join us on vacations and he was actually one of my largest clients at CES which got me to number two on the Forbes list. Miguel said Carlos had no family and he won't be missed as he continued to dispose of his body into the ocean. Miguel grabbed a fishing pole and attached the last piece to the hook and cast it out. That moment officially ruined fishing for me for the rest of my life.

I was washing off the deck of the boat and Miguel sat in his chair waiting for a bite. He landed a fish and pulled it up, no joke, he caught a large Bonefish. I saw several fish swimming around the boat and it disgusted me to my core. Miguel wanted to keep the fish and cook it when we got back to the island. I started the boat and before heading back Miguel said he would take Carlos's spot and become a client of mine at CES. He said his net worth was close to $3.3 Billion and he heard from Carlos (RIP) that I was the best, well second best, in the business. As we headed back to the island my assistant at CES called me and told me Dayana came through with a bunch of referrals from her tech friends. She said several were high profile CEO's and they wanted to invest with us and she told me how much that would bring in, roughly $5.3 Billion, I also did the math in my head and added Miguel's assets to my overall portfolio of clients and that easily put me at #1 on the Forbes list.

I was now a partner with one of the largest drug lords in the world and I would soon be number one on the Forbes list. If you've ever played the game "King of the Hill" where you try to knock off the person standing on top of the mound of dirt, at that very moment in my life it felt like that, like I knocked off my competition and I was standing at the top. I was King of the Hill as a Broker and a Dealer.

Chapter 10 – Plot Twist

When you're king of the hill that means everyone is trying to do everything they can to knock you off the top of hill. I tried to limit my interaction with Miguel but I had no choice but to stay engaged with him on a daily basis. I don't know what the hell Carlos was thinking because Miguel was paranoid, he even mentioned he had a few guys checking in on me periodically to make sure I wouldn't turn on him. Of course I would never do that as that would incriminate myself and be my own demise. I loved Dayana, Sara, James, and Tim too much to put them at risk so the only other option I had was to find a way out.

I was pulling in a lot of money and thought by now the Feds would be watching me but to my surprise they weren't, trust me Miguel had a sweep done periodically of my houses which we called "cleaning day" and we made it appear like a cleaning crew came once a week to clean my house. And with all of my dealers using my system of "intent to buy stocks" it appeared I was doing business all the time on every phone call and e-mail communication I made. Not once did I say or type the words, drugs, weed, marijuana, cocaine, ecstasy, or cannabis. I tried to be ten steps ahead of the Feds but I was worried about Miguel's visit to the island. What if they we're watching him and somehow saw me with him. I also thought back to his comment about Carlos' dealer ratting him out and what if they saw us boarding the private jet together in Miami. I could always say I was pursuing new clients for CES, but would they believe that, doubtful. I started to become paranoid myself.

I tried to maintain a normal life and spend as much time with my family as possible to portray the "All American Dream" lifestyle. We occasionally had lavish parties at the beach house and invited clients along with my top five dealers, which included Randy and Fred, both who I trusted the most. I told them not to sell while at the party but they could solicit interest for future prospects. Some clients brought their own goodies with them but if it didn't come from any of my guys then we couldn't get in trouble for it because they can't trace it back to me or Miguel.

Sara flew out from Colorado and stayed with us for a few days. She said she had important news, and told me she changed career direction and decided to become an agent for the DEA. She said one of her roommates in college overdosed on opioids and wanted to find the person who sold her the Oxy pills. She said she already had her first assignment and I told her that college is fully paid for if she decided to stay and she also has her Roth IRA to use when it comes time to buy a house or in case of emergencies. I also told her I would fully support whatever path she decided on, even though I was praying she would change her mind and want to come work for me as a Financial Advisor and take over my book of clients, but I was afraid she had no interest in Finance and there was no way I would ever bring her into my drug ring business.

Sara flew back to Colorado, or so I thought, and Dayana along with our new Au Pair and the boys flew to California for the weekend to see her brother. I was home by myself when I heard the intercom buss for the gate. I looked at the video from the camera feed and I noticed a large man with sunglasses in the driver's seat. I asked "how can I help you" and the large man said "I'm the driver for Miguel and he would like to speak to you in person". I thought what in the hell is he doing here, fuck! I pressed the button to open the gate and they drove up the driveway to the front door. Miguel got out of the large black Suburban and came towards me and leaned in to give me a hug. I said "Hi Miguel, what brings you here? Would you like to go over your investment portfolio?" just in case he was tapped or someone was watching, and I welcomed him into the house. Miguel said he has some gifts for me and the giant of a man with him brought in four large duffle bags which appeared to be full of something. He set them down in the middle of the living room. Miguel walked up to them and unzipped each one, all four filled with cash. I looked at Miguel and asked what I was supposed to do with all of it as my three safes were already full of cash, gold bars, and jewelry. He said having $60 Million in cash is a tough problem to have, each bag contained $15 Million each. I asked what it was for and how did he bring it into the states. Miguel told me he brought it up from Miami, said

Carlos was holding onto it for him and there's a lot more where that came from. He said it was my half of the earnings from profits as we are now partners. I said "Wow, that's a lot for a year" and he laughed and said "no gringo, this is your half of the money we made for the moth, and every month I'll continue to bring you your share of the profits, partner".

Since Dayana was out of town, I decided to invite Miguel to stay for dinner and took him downtown to a place called River and Post. As we looked out over the Saint Johns River, Miguel turned to me and said he had to tell me something important. He said there's other cartels out there that wanted his head on a platter and he planned to stay in Miami for a bit. He said as a partner, I had to be aware of the risk involved just in case anyone ever found out we were partners, and if that ever happened I'd have a bounty on my head as well. He said he was glad he could trust me because without trust, all of this would go to shit.

The very next day I got a call from Sara, thanking me for being so supportive and she said she had officially joined the Drug

Enforcement Agency and she was stationed in Bogota working on her first assignment. My heart just dropped and I was so scared for my baby girl, not to mention the irony of the matter. She said she loved it and was excited about the job but she apologized because she couldn't give me details on the assignment they were working on. I just knew it was close to Medellin, which is where Miguel's farm was located. She said if I watched the news later I would see what she's working on. I told her to please be VERY careful and that I'd watch the news, then we hung up the phone.

Just then Miguel walked in the room holding his phone. He was pissed off about something and I thought to myself, oh shit, he tapped my call and just heard me talking to Sara who's now in the DEA and he's going to think I'm working with her, he's going to shoot me in the head like he did Carlos. I started thinking about Dayana, Sara, and the boys, and Miguel said "I just got a call for my associate in Medellin and the fucking Feds burned down my entire farm, those putas". I had a look of shock and said "the whole farm? How did they find it?" and Miguel was shaking his head back and forth and said "I have no idea, maybe Carlos was talking to the Feds". I assured him Carlos hadn't said a word but I thought to myself, how could I be sure about that, but I couldn't. If he did, then I'm in deep shit unless he didn't mention anything about me. Miguel said we're going to have to rebuild the farm, but this time we have to use my island.

I turned the TV on to watch the news like Sara had suggested and at that moment I told Miguel maybe this was a sign that we need to get out altogether, that we both have enough money to last several lifetimes, he looked at me with disgust and said "you want out gringo, the only way…" then the news popped on and it showed the story about the burning of one of Columbia's largest Cannabis and Cocaine farms, then a DEA agent appeared, you couldn't see her full face as she wore a black mask over her mouth and nose, she also had a DEA hat on but I could see her eyes and that was definitely Sara. Miguel said "you want out…well just like that fucking bitch, when I find out who she is, it'll be in a body bag for the both of you".

I told Miguel I was just throwing it out there and I wasn't planning on leaving, the money is good but it's going to take a long time to get back up and running. Miguel said we can use the farms I have in Colorado and Massachusetts to bridge the gap until we get the farm on Water Caye up and running. I thought to myself, the only way I can get out of this by killing Miguel myself. I couldn't hire someone as they could be undercover and I couldn't turn him in without doing time myself, so I had only one solution. I planned it in my head, I would take him fishing on Randy's charter boat and do it while we're 30 miles out in the Atlantic with no one around us. Let the sharks have at him just like he did Carlos.

It was Saturday night and I asked Miguel to stay one more day and I told his driver, the big guy, that Miguel and I would fly back to Miami later. I called Dayana and asked her to fly to Telluride and I'd meet her and the boys there on Tuesday. I got up early Sunday to take the four large duffle bags full of cash, $60 Million, to a property I owned in Springfield where I decided to bury the money. I took photos of where I hid the money using

Dayana's app, 1K, so I wouldn't forget where it was buried. I created a public album (Album Code: SPRIN466995) and I added the album to the map, that way I could type the album name, Springfield, in the search bar at the top of the map and it would show me where the money was hidden. Just in case something happened to me I could send the album link/code with a note to Dayana to let her know where to find the money.

When I got home, I logged into work for a bit to check some e-mails before heading out with Miguel. I was listed as the top Financial Advisor in the US. I picked up a few more Super High Net Worth clients, Top Ranked Athletes and a few high profile movie Directors, I definitely wanted out of this bullshit as Dayana and I made way more money than either of us could ever spend. I don't know why I was so greedy and became such a money hungry shallow prick, but I realized the errors of my ways and it was time to end it with Miguel. I needed to find a gun and then I remembered, Randy always has one on the boat right next to the Captain's Chair in the box below the steering wheel. I called Randy and asked if he still had the gun,

I said I wanted to be safe, just in case. Randy said he had one on the boat and I shouldn't worry so much, he said "what are you, paranoid". Go figure, I'm one of the largest drug dealers in the US and I've never owned or held a gun in my life.

I told Miguel we're going fishing and I planned the entire day for us. He said he loves fishing and he laughed and said "we need some bait, got any dead bodies lying around here" which took me back to the time he shot Carlos and it pissed me off and made me focus on what a horrible person he really was. We boarded the boat with Randy and I introduced them to each other. I told Miguel that Randy was my top producer in Jacksonville. With Randy there it gave a sense of legitimacy and Miguel had no idea what my intentions were. Miguel was busy getting his fishing rod set up so I pulled Randy aside and told him what we had to do and I asked if he brought the gun with him, Randy told me he has it but he's not taking part in any of it, that he never signed up for that. Randy said I would have to figure out another date and time as today wasn't the day. We were 30 miles out and not a single boat near us, several cargo boats were way off in the distance, so I waited for the right time when Randy was away from the Captain's Chair and I grabbed the gun and put it in my pants behind my back.

Randy was helping Miguel bait his line and I pulled the gun out and pointed it at Randy and said "I'm on to you, you piece of shit" and Miguel and Randy looked at me and Randy had a look of fear. I told Randy to step away from Miguel and I said "I know you're working with the Feds" and all the sudden Miguel pulled out his gun and pointed it at Randy and said "are you the mother fucker that sold us out?", just then I had to think fast before Miguel shot Randy so I quickly turned to Miguel and pulled the trigger. My shot hit its target but not before Miguel got a shot off himself and it grazed Randy's shoulder. Miguel fell overboard and was bleeding out as I shot him right in the chest. He went under water and never came back up. Randy looked at me and said "what the fuck was that, you asshole, I could have been killed". I said "I told you, Miguel's crazy and he was planning to kill us both which is why I had to do what I did, it was either him or us". I don't know if Randy believed me but all the sudden I felt like a huge weight had been lifted and I was free, free to get out of the drug dealing bullshit and I could now focus on my family and my clients. I helped Randy clean his wound and I apologized profusely knowing Randy was engaged to Candy, real name Mandy, yes Randy and Mandy. I felt horrible, Miguel could have shot him in the head like he did Carlos and it would have been my fault.

We got back to Mayport and docked the boat and I took Randy out for drinks and told him the entire story. How I got into all of this bullshit just so I could afford to pay Lisa for child support, how Sara had become an agent for DEA and was getting close to our operation which is why I needed to get out before she suspected my involvement. Plus with two little boys, I wanted to focus more time on Dayana and help her out more around the house, even though we had an Au Pair who lived with us full time. Randy understood and even said he was thinking about getting out as well but wasn't sure how to tell me. We held up our beers and said "cheers, we had a good run".

Chapter 11 – Dilemma

I called Dayana and asked her and the boys to fly back home instead of going to Telluride, change of plans. Then I pulled all of my suppliers and dealers together, on a conference call, and told them what had happened "due to the recent volatility of the market, we're no longer soliciting interest in any of the recommended stocks on the list we provided you. I suggest you find a new Advisor to purchase stocks from as I will no longer be taking on new clients from this day forward". I hung up the phone and I was done, finally out of the game.

My assistant came into my office and handed me my itinerary for tomorrow, New York, as I was the key note speaker at a conference hosted by several large investment firms in New York, crap I forgot about that trip. I left work and got home just as Dayana and the boys got home, we had dinner and I put the boys to bed. It was 9:30 and Dayana just slipped into some sexy lingerie and was pulling me into bed as my flight left early the next morning, and I was just about to make love to my beautiful wife when my cell phone rang, it was Sara. I was worried about her so I told Dayana it would have to wait a minute. I answered the phone and said "hey Sara, is everything ok?" and she said she was going to fly back to Florida because she wants to meet with me to talk about something personal. I said we can talk now and she said she wanted to talk face to face because it's important.

I thought maybe she had met someone or was possibly pregnant based on the urgency but then my mind wondered back to Miguel and I was scared it might be related to that. She told me she was flying back in a few days and I told her that was perfect as I'll be back from New York by then. She said "Dad, I love you" and then she hung up the phone.

I went back to the bedroom and Dayana was there waiting for me, naked in bed. She asked if everything was ok with Sara and I said she was going to come visit in a few days. I couldn't stop thinking it was about the drugs and I lost all interest in sex and couldn't perform. Dayana asked if everything was ok but I made an excuse that my mind was on the speech for tomorrow and I was actually nervous about it which must be why I can't perform. Dayana said "you can always take a pill" and I told her it's probably best to just call it a night and I would make it up to her when I got back from New York.

I flew up to New York and landed at JFK and took a private car into the city. I went straight to the conference, gave my speech and instead of staying the night I changed my plans and flew right back to Jacksonville. I was nervous about Sara's phone call and I wanted to get everything in order just in case, planning for the worst. I liquidated some assets, as much as possible, and transferred as many securities as I could without looking to suspicious over to Dayana's single name account. I took the cash I withdrew to the same location in Springfield where I buried the $60 Million in the four duffle bags.

I got home and Dayana called from her office and asked why I made such a large transfer to her account. I said happy Anniversary honey. I know you want to invest in more tech startups so I decided to move over some securities to your account. She surprisingly bought it and said I'll see you tomorrow when you get home from New York and I told her I was sorry because I forgot to call her to tell her I was coming back early. I told her Sara was coming home in a few days and I wanted to get a few things in order in case she needs access to her Roth IRA as it sounded like she had an urgent matter and I wanted to make her aware of her Roth, as I never fully covered it with her. Dayana said she was excited I was back early and she whispered on the phone "plus we can continue what we started last night". We hung up the phone and I began to write Dayana a letter explaining everything and how truly sorry I was for getting her and the whole family involved in that world and taking it as far as I did. I apologized to her and the kids for being a money hungry dick and I was extremely selfish. I tried to explain how I thought about getting out for her and the kids, but I was already in way over my head and I couldn't get out without being killed by Miguel or someone else. I told her I originally got into it because I owed Lisa a lot of money in child support at the time but that doesn't justify why I stayed in it when I could have got out. I hid the letter in my desk drawer and decided that if anything happened to me I would tell her where it was.

Dayana got home and she wasn't lying, she wanted to continue what we started last night and it was probably the most passionate sex we have ever had as I was still nervous about Sara's visit. As we laid in bed, Dayana curled up on me, she asked if everything was ok and asked if there was anything I needed to tell her. I tried to play it off as Sara having big news that she wouldn't say over the phone and I was just nervous for her and hoped everything was ok. I said I was moving funds around to diversify our portfolio and wanted to liquidate some of the lesser performing assets. She also bought that and told me the great news about her app, they hit record earnings and were about to go public. They were even creating a crypto currency called 1K Coin and used blockchain advertising which paid users in crypto currency to click on ads and view videos related to the content regarding the events they were hosting or attending. She said they also acquired the AR Company she invested in and they were working to add AR filters to 1K photo albums in order to compete with other apps. At that moment my heart broke because I thought about how much shame I was going to bring her if Sara has me thrown in jail. She's ranked as the #1 CEO in Tech and she'll be crushed all because I'm an idiot.

Sara called that evening and said she would be by the house first thing in the morning instead and that we needed to speak privately. I told her Dayana would be at work and the nanny will have the boys, so we can speak privately. The next morning I woke up early, nervous about Sara's visit. I ran into my office and I added the 1K album code (SPRIN466995) to the letter showing Dayana exactly where I hid the money, and told her to dig it up in case of an emergency. Sara arrived and Dayana had already left for work and the boys were out with the Au Pair. I went out to the driveway and I gave Sara a big hug and she hugged me back but not as hard as she usually does. We walked inside and she said "Dad, we need to talk".

We went into my office and I closed the door. Sara sat in the chair across from my desk and I sat down at my desk. I looked at her and said "so what's going on pumpkin?" and Sara said "Dad, I know all about your involvement with Carlos and Miguel". I nodded my head and didn't say a word, in my mind I was freaking out because it was about to all come crashing down on me and she could see the look on my face and she continued "I know Dad, but" she paused for a long moment pondering whether to continue "but no one else knows Dad. We were investigating Miguel and we followed him from his farm to Belize and then he got on a boat and went to an island but we lost him and we didn't know which one. I put it together because you were at Water Caye at the exact same time with Carlos. We watched the tapes at the Miami airport and I saw Carlos walking with a guy. The camera couldn't get a good shot of you but I checked your calendar and you were in Miami at that very same time picking up a friend before flying out to Belize. I haven't said anything to my superiors, yet. I know it's you because I also called Mom to ask her how much you paid in child support and she said you paid way more than the court ordered amount. So I put two and two together and knew you had to be making extra money on the side since I was a baby. Just be honest with me, is it you?"

I looked into her eyes and told her everything, even the part about me having to kill Miguel to get out of it. I told her why I did it and I apologized from the bottom of my heart. I said I'm sorry for putting her in this position and I tried to explain how it was all over and I was finally out, but Sara said she had to report everything because I broke the law. She started to cry and I got up to hug her and she pushed me away and said "you brought this on yourself and I'm sorry Dad but you have to suffer the consequences of your actions" then she ran out of the house and jumped in her rental car and drove off.

My hands were shaking and I thought for sure I'd have the DEA at my door any minute. I gathered everything I could think of that had value; jewelry, the gold bars, paintings, everything in my three safes and I loaded all of it into the C-Class and drove it to my spot in Springfield and added that to everything else I had buried there. As I drove back to the house I thought about Sara and how tough it must have been for her to decide whether or not to throw your own father in jail. I tried to call her but she didn't answer. I arrived home and the Au Pair was back with the boys and Dayana returned home.

I went to my office and grabbed the letter and I shared the album code via the app to Dayana's phone. I took Dayana upstairs and handed her the letter and she asked me what the album was I sent her. I told her to sit down and I began to explain everything and told her to shred the letter. Dayana sat there in silence with a look of complete and utter disbelief as it all sunk in, I could see she was angry. She stood up, we were face to face and she slapped me hard. She said "how could you, you piece of shit, what the fuck were you thinking" she walked into the closet and grabbed her suit case and said "I'm taking the boys to California because they don't need to be here when Sara has you arrested. Oh and by the way, we're getting divorced you lying, selfish, prick. Lisa was smart not to marry you" then she left with the nanny and the boys.

I sat in my house, all alone, waiting, thinking about everything that has happened and wishing I had a time machine to go back and stop myself from making the call to Todd. I wish I would have taken the hard but honest route and struggled to make child support payments for a few years until I made more money, but I have to live with my choices and as Sara said, I had to suffer the consequences of my actions. I kept waiting but no one ever came for me. I eventually fell asleep on the couch in the living room and I heard a car pull into the driveway. I thought here we go, so I got up and walked to the front door. I opened it expecting to see SWAT or the DEA, but instead there was a single shadowy figure and when they walked towards the house the light hit their face and it was Sara.

She came inside and we sat on the couch. She looked at me and said she's thought long and hard about it and she's not going to say anything to her boss. She said "I know what kind of impact this would have on Dayana, James, and Tim and I can't put them through that. If it's true what you said about being completely out of it and you promise me you are 100% done with all of that, then I'll keep your secret. Besides you're my Dad and I love you and I know you did it to help me and my Mom, and Dayana and the boys, and no one will ever find out because I also destroyed any evidence of your potential involvement". I sat there in tears and I leaned over and gave Sara a hug and a kiss on the cheek. I told her I was truly sorry, not just because I got caught, but I was sorry for putting her in that position and for putting the family at risk. I promised to never get involved in that shit again. I told her about the conversation I had with Dayana earlier and Sara said she apologized but that was the right thing to do and she would call her and explain everything and not to worry. I didn't mention the money I had buried to Sara and I felt bad about that, but I was also glad it was there just in case.

Sara went back to work for the DEA and kept getting promoted and eventually settled down with her husband in DC. Her Roth IRA paid for their wedding, two cars, brownstone in Georgetown, and had a lot left over for college for her daughter and son. Dayana divorced me and moved to San Francisco to run her app and was on the Board of Directors for several companies, her net worth is now over $4 Billion. We share custody of the boys and I'm still the number one Financial Advisor in the US, working for CES which had its greatest year ever and is now the largest Broker Dealer Firm in the world.

So who am I? I'm you, I'm a hard working American who's made some bad choices and had failures and success. I'm a Lawyer, Doctor, Fire Fighter, Startup CEO, or I could be your Financial Advisor at your local…Broker Dealer.